Coming Home

ANNIE SEATON

Duckinwilla Days: Book 1

Heartwarming and compelling tales of love, self-discovery, and second chances in the heart of rural Australia.

COMING HOME

This book is a work of fiction. Names, characters, places, magazines and incidents are the product of the author's imagination or are used fictitiously. Any resemblance to actual events, locales, or persons, living or dead, is coincidental.
Copyright © 2025 Annie Seaton

All rights reserved.

ISBN 9781923048621

ANNIE SEATON

The Johnson family

Grandmère and Papa: Margot and Robert Johnson

The parents: Hugo and Ellen Johnson

The Johnson siblings:

Charlotte Johnson - Book 1 - *Coming Home*

Julien Johnson - Book 2 - *Secrets and Surprises*

Oliver Johnson - Book 3 - *Wishes and Whispers*

Lisette Johnson - Book 4 - *New Beginnings*

Guy Johnson - Book 5 - *Chasing Dreams*

Amelia Johnson - Book 6 - *Together at Last*

COMING HOME

CHAPTER 1

Brisbane

The staffroom at Helen's Creek High smelled of chocolate and rang with farewells. Charlotte Johnson stared at the massive cake Rose was carrying through the doorway, its candles flickering like the warning signals in her mind. Another goodbye, another step further from home.

'Bushfire warning?' She forced a laugh, gesturing at the blazing candles.

'It's not that big.' Rose's brown eyes sparkled with mischief as she navigated between desks. 'Mandy, grab this before I recreate the Great Brisbane Cake Disaster of 2023.'

The familiar banter wrapped around Charlotte like the comfort "blanky" she'd had when she was a toddler. For two years, this Brisbane staffroom had been her refuge—the place where she'd rebuilt herself after fleeing Duckinwilla Creek. The thought of her hometown sent that familiar ache through her chest, one she'd learned to ignore.

'Last day,' Mandy announced, rescuing the cake from Rose's precarious grip. 'Last chance to change your mind about France.'

Charlotte's smile turned wistful. 'I know. I've had a fabulous two years working here with you guys. They never told me at uni that I'd laugh most of the day when I joined an English staffroom at a school.'

'It's not like that everywhere.' Rose shook her head. 'Mind you, I've worked in some pretty tough schools over the past ten years.'

Mandy nodded. 'Me too. My first appointment was a nightmare. The playground at Breakwater High was like a war zone during most breaks. You've had a gentle introduction, Charlotte.'

'I know, I've been very lucky. And I'm really going to miss you both. Who am I going to go to for advice now?'

Rose put a hand to her chest and pretended to swoon. 'Some gorgeous Frenchman, of course!'

Charlotte grinned at her. 'One can only hope.'

The trio of language teachers had forged a strong friendship since Charlotte arrived at

Helen's Creek High School in Brisbane two years ago. At first, Charlotte lacked confidence and was slow to respond, but Mandy and Rose were persistent. Their bond had seen them through both fun and challenging times, including the sudden passing of their head teacher at the end of Charlotte's first year.

The cake found its way to the centre of the table, chocolate ganache glistening in the fluorescent light. Around her, colleagues gathered, their chatter filling the room with warmth. She'd miss this, miss them. Miss belonging somewhere that didn't hurt.

'Come on, Charlotte. The candles are going to burn down if you don't hurry up.'

'I'm not expected to blow that fire out, am I?' Charlotte joked.

'Well, it's not going to go out by itself, and if you don't hurry up, it's going to burn down to that yummy chocolate ganache,' Mandy replied.

Cake always drew a crowd in the shared English and Language Department staffroom. Regret fluttered through her briefly, and she wondered if she was crazy to leave this school and head overseas to an unknown teaching environment. The staff here—and the majority of the students—were fabulous to work with. She pushed away the thought. Going to France had been a dream that Grandmère had fostered since Charlotte was a little girl.

Fifteen minutes later, empty paper plates littered the table. The remnants of the cake sat at an uneven angle, crumbs scattered over the bench.

'Mrs Barber makes the best cakes ever, doesn't she?' Mandy said, brushing the crumbs from the front of her dress.

'You can always depend on Mrs Barber,' Rose agreed. 'Mandy, you've got a chocolate moustache.'

Mandy raced to the small mirror near the door. She looked at her reflection and then pulled a face at Rose. 'I have not!'

Rose chuckled. 'You're so easy to wind up, Mandy.'

'So, heading off to the airport tomorrow, Charlie?' Rose asked.

'No,' she replied slowly. 'I've got some family stuff to do first. I don't fly out till the first week in January.'

'Gosh, it'll be cold in France then—middle of their winter! Crazy woman, leaving our beautiful summer,' Mandy teased.

'Listen, if you're not going for another three weeks, you might have time to come and join us up in the islands,' Rose suggested.

Charlotte shook her head. 'No, family duty calls.'

'You've never told us where you grew up.' Mandy's voice cut through her thoughts. 'Come on, Charlie. Last day—spill some secrets.'

Charlotte hesitated, then made a face. 'You wouldn't have heard of it.'

'Try us,' Rose said, a determined gleam in her eye.

'Yeah, come on—you've never told us where you grew up or went to school.'

'I'll bet you ten bucks you've never heard of it.' Charlotte grinned. She was going to miss this banter.

'You're on.' Rose folded her arms and waited.

'Little place south of Bundaberg. Sugarcane country.' The words tasted of childhood summers and broken promises. 'Duckinwilla Creek.'

Rose and Mandy exchanged glances, and Rose shook her head. 'I guess I owe you ten bucks.'

'I've never heard of it either,' Mandy said.

'I have.'

Charlotte's heart stumbled. Greg Barrett, their head of department, stood in the doorway, his presence filling the room the way it always did. She'd been fighting her attraction to him for months, telling herself it didn't matter—she was leaving anyway.

'My parents' farm's just over at Dunmora,' he continued, and Charlotte's world tilted slightly.

'Over the hills from us,' she managed, memories flooding back—summer storms rolling in across those same hills, the heavy sweetness of burnt cane on the wind, the way the creek water turned gold at sunset.

'Haven't been back lately?' His question was gentle, but Charlotte heard the curiosity beneath it.

'Five years.' She forced the words past the tightness in her throat. 'Not since before uni.'

'You've never told us you grew up on a farm, Charlotte,' Mandy said.

'Your last day at school, and we're learning more about you than we have in the last two years,' Rose added.

'It never came up in conversation.'

'Like you said, it's a small town,' Greg said. 'But it's become quite gentrified and touristy lately. The last time I was up there, I couldn't get over the change. Apparently, after COVID, the local chamber of commerce reinvigorated the town. Have you seen all the painted cows and sculptures that are through the town now, Charlotte? It's become quite arty.'

Charlotte shook her head. 'I really don't know, Greg. I haven't been out there for a long time.' Changing the subject, Charlotte turned to Greg. 'Where are you headed for the holidays?'

His slow smile made her pulse skip.

'Funny thing—France. My sister lives there.'

'What a coincidence.' Rose's voice dripped with innocence that fooled no one. 'Near Lyon, Greg?'

Heat crept up Charlotte's neck as Greg nodded.

'We'll have to meet for coffee,' he said, and something in his voice made her look up, catching his gaze.

'Oh . . . well . . . um, yes, that would be nice.'

Heat rushed into her face as she stumbled over her words. She swallowed the regret that rose. Development of this attraction was something she couldn't afford to consider. Not now, not when she was finally escaping. Not when home was calling her back first, in the form of Grandmère's letter burning a hole in her bag.

Come home, ma petite. *It's time to face the past.*

Charlotte pushed away the little flare of attraction that was becoming way too frequent lately. Greg was a fine-looking man and had led the department well. She'd never heard him say a cross word or anything negative. He'd made a difference to the culture in the staffroom.

She didn't miss the knowing look that Mandy and Rose exchanged.

CHAPTER 2

Duckinwilla Creek

Julien Johnson's attention was not on the town like it usually was as he drove down the main street of Duckinwilla Creek towards his grandparents' house. In his role as president of the Chamber of Commerce, he usually kept a close eye on the main street. Their new home sat on top of the rise, looking over the small township to the east and the valley to the west. The house that had been his grandparents' home when he had been a child was now sitting empty, and no matter how often the family encouraged them to sell it, Grandmère refused to part with it.

'Our Charlotte loves that house, and one day she will live there.' No matter that she'd lived in Duckinwilla Creek since she'd fallen in love with an Aussie boy and followed him to Australia in her twenties, Grandmère's accent was pronounced. 'And don't you look at me like that, Lisette,' she chastised her granddaughter. 'You will all get your fair share when our time comes.'

'I wasn't going to say anything, Grandmère.'

Julien had kept silent, too. Lisette had been in a foul mood ever since Mum had announced that Charlotte was coming home and they would be holding a farewell function for her.

Lisette had been vocal. 'That's ridiculous. We haven't seen her for five years, now she's coming home for a day or two, and you're giving her a party? I didn't even get a party for my twenty-first.' She flounced out of the living room before anyone could reply.

The setting sun painted Duckinwilla Creek's main street in shades of amber and gold as he passed their store, but Julien barely noticed. The pretty picture of the refurbished buildings bathed in the golden light failed to settle him. The stores, the bright flower baskets and the inviting aroma filling the street from the bakery in the family's store failed to lift his mood. All the sight of the General Store did this evening was bring back the tensions simmering between his siblings.

He was looking forward to Charlotte's return, but he was worried about the reception she'd get from the rest of the family. Even Mum and Dad hadn't seemed pleased to hear their eldest daughter was coming home, and that made him sad. On top of his other worries, Julien had to deal with this one.

Their dad, Hugo, was Grandmère and Papa's only son, but he and their mum, Ellen, had produced a brood of six children. Theirs had been a happy family unit until five years ago. There had been much change since the money had been stolen from the store. Dad had gone to work the farm with Oliver and Guy when the long-term manager had retired. To his surprise, Dad had asked Julien to take over the store, and he'd enjoyed every day he'd worked there and was proud of the changes he'd made.

Bloody Lisette. This situation was all her fault, and she was the one who harped on about it and bad-mouthed Charlotte every chance she got. No wonder Charlotte had stayed away for so long.

As he parked his ute at the end of the narrow laneway leading to the unique French provincial house on the side of the hill, Julien tried to shake off his bad mood. The new place was always referred to as Grandmère's house, despite Papa living there too. Grandmère cherished her role as the matriarch of the family, and he just hoped she could keep everyone in order tonight. Charlotte was arriving tomorrow, so he had no doubt what the summons to dinner was about.

Walking along the cobblestoned pathway leading to the house, he took a deep breath, trying to steady his nerves. The residence that Papa had built for his wife when he'd retired stood as a striking anomaly amidst the sugar cane farms with their old weatherboard Queenslanders; its symmetrical stone facades and tall, arched windows exuded old-world French charm. The lavender bushes lining the path released their fragrance, a subtle nod to the French heritage Grandmère cherished. As he approached the entrance, the ornate chandeliers inside cast a warm glow through the arched windows, illuminating the rich tapestries that adorned the walls. There was no doubt that Grandmère certainly had an eye for colour and design.

With a final, steadying breath, Julien opened the double cedar doors and stepped into Grandmère's *salon*. He knew the family meeting would be tense, with issues rehashed as they always were when the family got together.

Grandmère was trying to ease the way for Charlotte's return, but knowing his family, there would be raised voices tonight as everyone tried to give their opinion. But always positive, Julien held onto a sliver of hope that Charlotte's return might start to heal the rift that had fractured the family for more than five years.

'Julien! You are late.' His grandmother's voice hinted at her displeasure.

'Sorry, everyone. I was late closing the store. A busy afternoon.'

Truth be told, he'd dawdled. Any minute now, Lisette would start up about Charlotte again, and he was tired of being the referee. He hurried across the room where his grandparents, parents, two brothers and two of his three sisters sat at the dining room table. After kissing Grandmère's cheek and squeezing Papa's shoulder, he took his place beside Dad and smiled at Mum, who sat on the other side of the table with the girls. Guy and Oliver were talking quietly—no doubt about the cane harvest, as that was their main focus these days since Dad had handed the farm over to his sons. Lisette, wearing her perpetual scowl, and Amelia, sneaking glances at her phone. Only one empty chair, the one that had been vacant for five years.

Amelia looked up and caught Julien's eye,

and he frowned at her. There would be enough discussion tonight without a rant about mobile phones.

'Put it away,' he mouthed.

She nodded and leaned down, putting it away.

Grandmère stood and tapped a silver spoon on the side of a crystal wine glass. Her dark eyes gleamed with steely resolve as she addressed the family.

'Now that Julien is *finally* here, we shall talk about the next two weeks. Charlotte's return is imminent, and I expect *each* of you to treat her with the respect she deserves. Every one of you. She is family, and our family bond is unbreakable. The time for resolution is long overdue.'

Dad's jaw tightened, his weathered hands clenching the edge of the table. '*Maman*, it's not that simple. Charlotte's actions created the situation, and she left us all to deal with the fallout.'

'Created the situation?' Julien couldn't help himself. 'Or is it that we all chose to believe one side of the story?' He had defended Charlotte's actions on countless occasions, but everyone wanted to judge her and not the hard-done-by Lisette. If it weren't for the store, he and Emily would leave town, too.

Couldn't they see how unfair they were being? Charlotte had been hurt, but everyone had listened to Lisette.

'Here we go again.' Lisette's voice dripped with disdain. 'Saint Charlotte can do no wrong.'

'That's enough.' Papa's voice cut through the brewing argument. Despite marrying his French love, he was as direct as any farmer in the valley. 'Our granddaughter, your daughter, your sister will be here tomorrow. And you'll all be kind to her. Got that?'.

Mum's voice wavered; her frustration was evident. 'Charlotte was the one who chose to leave Duckinwilla Creek.'

'And left her family,' Lisette chimed in. 'With all respect, Grandmère, this farewell party you're planning is stupid.'

Uh-oh. No one called Grandmère stupid and got away with it.

Grandmere's gaze settled on Lisette. Everyone waited.

She straightened her posture and folded her hands elegantly on her lap before responding.

'Lisette,' she began, her tone measured. 'I appreciate honesty when it is tempered with thoughtfulness. However, to dismiss the planned farewell—a gesture of respect for your sister—as "stupid" displays a lack of discernment. Such words, my dear, should be chosen with greater care if you wish them to carry the weight of wisdom rather than a lack of thought.'

Julien kept his voice calm when Lisette jumped to her feet. 'Sit down, Lisette, and get over the attitude. And if you think about it, whatever happened, Charlotte would have left home anyway to go to uni. It was the attitude here that's kept her away for so long. And this attitude has hung around for far too long.'

Lisette, her dark eyes flashing with indignation, sat down and glared at her brother. 'Attitude? You expect me to welcome her back with open arms after what she did? She acted like she was better than us, and now we're supposed to forget and forgive all that?'

The silence that followed was heavy, with five years of hurt and misunderstanding. Through the windows, Julien could see the cane fronds waving in the gathering dusk. Somewhere out there was the childhood they'd all shared before secrets and accusations had torn them apart.

Oliver, his youngest brother, leaned forward, his expression serious. 'Lisette, maybe it's time to move on. You've let this blow up out of all proportion. You're obsessed with making Charlotte the baddie in this, and she's not even been here to defend herself.'

'*She* was in the wrong,' Lisette said.

Guy shook his head. 'Oliver's right. Charlotte is coming home, and I, for one, think she's very brave to be doing that. I mean, how many of you have talked to her in the last few months? She always sends us birthday cards, and those of us who call her know how lonely she's been.'

'Pffft,' Lisette spluttered.

Amelia glared at her sister. 'I remember how much happier we all were before she left. I miss that. I miss us being a family. A happy family. Look at us now. All arguing, and she's not even here. She's had little to do with us over the past five years, and she's never said a cross word to any of us when she's called, has she, Mum? Charlotte is mature enough to have moved on.'

'And are you saying that I'm not?' Lisette's

voice was shrill.

'If the cap fits,' Guy muttered.

'Mum!' Lisette turned to her mother for support, and Ellen went to speak.

'Enough!' Grandmère's gaze swept over her family. 'We cannot change the past, but we can choose how we move forward. Charlotte's return is a chance to mend what has been broken. I ask you all to consider what kind of family we wish to be. Attitude is a good word, Julien. I would ask you to think deeply about yours, Lisette.'

Lisette's face flushed with anger, her hands trembling. 'This is unbelievable. You're all so quick to welcome her back and forget how she made us feel. Well, I won't be a part of this charade.'

Dad sighed deeply, rubbing his temples. 'This is exactly what I was afraid of with her coming home. As hard as it sounds, Charlotte would have been better off not coming home before she went to France.'

Julien placed a reassuring hand on his father's shoulder. 'No, Dad. It's going to be hard, but we owe it to Charlotte.'

His mother dabbed at her eyes with a handkerchief. 'It's gone too far, and it's gone on too long. She has caused the damage.'

'We all have our flaws.' Grandmère's voice was gentle yet firm. 'We must be willing to listen, to forgive *each other* despite them.' Her glare settled on Lisette.

'You realise that she's only going to France to get in your good books, Grandmère.' Lisette returned the glare as Mrs Hyslop appeared with the first course, the familiar scent of garlic a counterpoint to the tension around the table. Julien watched his family—his mother's trembling hands on her cup, his father's distant gaze, Amelia's hopeful eyes.

The once-heated discussion gradually gave way to a fragile peace; everyone was lost in their own thoughts, worrying about Charlotte's return and wondering what tomorrow would bring.

Julien broke the silence as coffee was served, his voice steady. 'So, do we all agree? Charlotte's return is a chance to put the past away once and for all?'

His parents put their heads down and focused on their coffee. He gave them the benefit of the doubt. Maybe they thought he hadn't included them in the question.

Oliver nodded. 'Yes, we'll be here for

Charlotte.' He turned to Lisette with his eyebrows raised, but she put her head down and ignored him.

Guy gave Julien a thumbs-up.

Amelia looked up, her eyes filled with a mixture of hope and apprehension. 'I want to know my big sister. I don't want her to go to France and never come home again.'

Her words hung in the air. Outside, a magpie called its evening song, and somewhere in the distance, a dog barked. Just another night in Duckinwilla Creek, except nothing about tomorrow would be ordinary.

Charlotte was coming home, and none of them were ready for what that meant.

CHAPTER 3

Maison de Rêve

The crunch of gravel under Charlotte's feet seemed too loud in the evening stillness. She eased her car door shut, heart thudding as she faced her grandparents' old home. *Maison de Rêve*—house of dreams. The name felt like poetry, dreams and memories tangled together.

She was pretty sure no one lived here now but was prepared to be surprised. Communication in the Johnson family had been fragmented since the big blow-up the weekend before she left home five years ago.

Maison de Rêve stood proud against the darkening sky, its weathered facade telling stories of fifty years of Johnson family life. Papa had built this, their first home, with his own hands when Grandmère followed him home from her tiny French village, trading Beaune's vineyards for Queensland's cane fields. She had loved listening to Grandmère's stories of spending her childhood in the small village. Margot had never dreamed of leaving her village, nestled in the heart of the *Côte d'Or* vineyards, until a handsome Aussie came to work on the vines, and she fell in love with him.

Charlotte walked to the edge of the lawn, drinking in the vista below. Someone was keeping the grounds neat—the grass clipped short, the garden beds weeded—though there weren't as many flowers as when Grandmère had tended them. Charlotte had inherited Grandmère's love of gardening. For a short while, before she'd started her teaching degree, she'd toyed with the idea of studying horticulture. She closed her eyes and took a deep breath, inhaled the sweet fragrance of lavender, and pushed away the uncertainty about returning to her hometown.

Charlotte turned and walked across the gravel towards the front door, pushing away the nerves that were making her legs feel shaky. She reached into the cavity behind the weathered frog sculpture and nodded as her fingers closed around the big brass key.

Focus on the good memories—the days when her grandparents lived in *Maison de Rêve. When everyone was happy.*

Walking to the door, she hesitated. She still

wasn't ready for this, for the memories she knew would rush in and overwhelm her. But she had come to say goodbye—not just to *Maison de Rêve*, or the town, but to the life she had once had here. The life she'd foolishly believed to be her future. It was time to move on once and for all. She'd foolishly thought that five years away would have restored her strength, but no, the nerves skittering in her stomach proved her wrong.

The door creaked open, and the musty smell of disuse greeted her. Dust motes danced in the last rays of sunlight streaming through the picture window, settling on surfaces that had once gleamed with Grandmère's careful attention. She closed her eyes, remembering the happy days she'd spent here in her childhood. Curled up with Grandmère on the window seat, learning French when she was still at primary school, playing chase with Papa around the sofa as he pretended to be a bear, happy family dinners around the massive timber dining room table that had obviously been moved to the new house. Charlotte hadn't seen their new house on the other side of town yet, but Grandmère had told her all about it in her weekly calls. She had been the one constant connection to home.

Charlotte dropped her bag by the door and crossed to the window seat. She ran her fingers over the sill, leaving trails in the dust with her fingertips.

Duckinwilla Creek Valley stretched out below, patchwork fields gilded by sunset. How many times had she sat here with Grandmère, learning French verbs and family stories? How many times had she watched Papa chase her siblings around the massive timber dining table that now lived in their new house?

Charlotte stood at the window until darkness crept across the valley and the town's lights began to twinkle like earthbound stars. Her reflection in the glass stared back at her, pale and tired. Teaching French at the high school in Brisbane had kept her busy, given her new friends and a new life, but she still hadn't regained the trust she'd lost here. Coming back to Duckinwilla Creek was like reopening an old wound, but she knew she had to do it—shedding that layer of family before stepping into a new chapter of her life.

An exciting new chapter. One that she would seize with both hands.

She opened the sliding door to let in the crisp evening air and locked the screen door. As darkness crept across the valley, she stood at the window again, gazing into the darkness. She wasn't sure how she felt. Strange was one word that came to mind.

The old house was familiar, but coming here after those years away felt different. Memories of growing up in Duckinwilla Creek flooded her mind: her mother's laughter, her brothers' teasing, her sisters' whispered secrets late at night. The French names her father had insisted on—Julien, Oliver, Guy, Lisette, and Amelia—were a constant reminder of their heritage. Grandmère had brought a piece of France with her when she had married Papa in the nineteen sixties and passed it on to Dad. The whole time, one question echoed in her mind: *What am I doing here? I should have gone straight to France.*

Her family didn't want her, so why had she jumped to Grandmère's summons?

For now, she'd push her worry aside. There would be time to deal with the family drama later. Tonight, she would let the quiet of the hills lull her to sleep.

With a determined sigh, Charlotte headed out to the car to bring in her overnight bag and then made her way upstairs to the room she had always slept in when Grandmère and Papa had lived here.

Upstairs, her old room waited exactly as she'd left it five years ago. Clean sheets on the bed—Grandmère's touch, she knew—and the same goose-down mattress that had cradled her through final exam study sessions. Back then, this room had been her sanctuary from the chaos of five siblings at home. It was almost as if it had been kept ready for her now despite the rest of the house being dusty.

A huge yawn overtook her, and she looked at the bed, which beckoned. She had a quick wash in the adjacent powder room, wiped her face with the flannel in her toiletries bag, slipped on her pyjamas, and climbed into the soft bed. As she slipped between crisp sheets, the sweet scent of lavender drifted in across the balcony and through the open door. The fragrance was one thing that always reminded her of home, and when she could find a bunch of lavender in Brisbane, Charlotte would buy it and place it on her desk at school.

She stared into the darkness, remembering the girl who'd dreamed of France in this very bed. She'd loved growing up at Duckinwilla Creek and loved her family with a fierceness that made her estrangement so difficult to bear.

One incident. That's all it had taken to shatter their harmony. As always, Charlotte knew she was overthinking, and she tried to breathe deeply, trying to compose herself. Overthinking the family situation was making her feel sick to her stomach, and she was stressed about seeing all of them tomorrow, even Grandmère, who had been her staunch supporter. The knowledge that her parents hadn't believed in her still cut deep.

Now Lyon beckoned with its six-month teaching contract, offering escape or opportunity—she wasn't sure which.

Spending time here with Grandmère had given her an interest in all things French; she had made French history a major in her degree, and her dream had always been to go to France to teach, and now that was about to happen. She lay back in bed and closed her eyes as the darkness cocooned her.

But as sleep pulled her under, carried on

waves of lavender-scented air, Charlotte wondered: *where was home now?'*

CHAPTER 4

Maison de Rêve

Charlotte woke as the first fingers of dawn filtered through the open cedar doors. For a moment, the years fell away and she was eighteen again, full of dreams and certainty. She opened her eyes and stretched, feeling calm and rested; she would not let that heavy ache return to her chest. And she would not worry about the reception from her family.

If they didn't want to resolve the ongoing situation—a ridiculous situation for which she took no blame—she would go to France, make a go of it, and maybe she would stay there for a lot longer.

If she didn't like it there, she'd find another school somewhere closer to home, not necessarily in Queensland. Perhaps she needed to see more of Australia.

Charlotte climbed out of bed and walked up the hallway to the bathroom. There was nothing in there; perhaps Grandmère hadn't prepared the room for her after all. She walked down the hall and opened the linen cupboard, but it was empty.

She had all her toiletries in her bag but hadn't thought to pack a towel. She grabbed her soap and shampoo from her bag, took a quick shower, and washed her hair. At least she had a hairdryer. By the time she stood in front of the mirror drying her hair, she had no need for a towel, and she walked out onto the small balcony to let the sun dry her skin, goosebumps rising on her bare flesh. She took a deep breath of the clean, fresh valley air.

I love this place.

The morning air held a hint of December chill as she stood, letting the sun warm her skin. Below, Duckinwilla Creek was starting to stir.

The sky was cloudless, and the heat wouldn't take long to build as the sun rose higher. She walked back into the room and made the bed before she turned to her bag and pulled out the dress she was going to wear to meet her family.

Once she pulled the bright yellow dress dotted with large red poppies over her head, Charlotte walked back into the bathroom and looked in the mirror. All she needed now was a bit of makeup, and she would look like the totally confident and happy woman she intended to present to her family. She reached for her brush and brushed her hair, then twisted it into a loose chignon before she found the red lipstick that matched the poppies in her dress. With one last satisfied look in the mirror—she looked very different from the eighteen-year-old who had left here—she nodded, turned, and went back to her bag to put everything away.

For a moment, she stood there, wondering whether to take the bag with her or to stay here again tonight. The only thing she'd need to bring back would be a towel. She shook her head. No, that was the coward's way out. If things got nasty, she would stay at Grandmère and Papa's new house; there would always be a welcome there.

She picked up her bag, headed downstairs, and locked the door behind her before she went to her car.

##

Duckinwilla Creek

The gravel crunched beneath the tyres as her small Audi navigated the winding road leading into town. A cloud of red-brown dust billowed behind her, settling stubbornly on the sleek black paint. She smiled to herself, imagining Julien's expression when he saw her car. He'd always dreamed of travelling, escaping the work of the family sugarcane farm, yet his loyalty to Dad had kept him tethered to Duckinwilla Creek.

Charlotte slowed as she passed the family farm where she had spent her childhood. The sign above the gate, *La Rêverie*, Dad's acknowledgment of his mother's French heritage, stood framed by lush greenery. The sugarcane fields swayed gently in the morning breeze, their bright green stalks vibrant against the windbreak of she-oaks.

In the distance, she spotted a truck parked by the machinery shed. The rhythmic sound of the harvester drifted faintly across the fields as it sliced through the tall stalks, reducing them to manageable lengths. Behind the harvester, a train engine waited on narrow tracks, its wagons lined with wire cages ready to transport the cane to the local mill.

She glanced around, half-expecting to see Julien directing operations from his usual spot by the shed, but there was no sign of him. Her three brothers—Julien, Oliver and Guy—had worked the farm since Papa retired just before Charlotte left home. Mum and Dad ran the family store in town.

Charlotte took a deep breath. She'd go there to see them; the store would be open by now. At least no one could make a scene in front of customers.

Shaking off the thought, she continued along the road toward town. She would see the rest of the family before she left—maybe. For now, she wanted to reconnect with Duckinwilla Creek on her own terms.

The landscape gradually shifted as she neared the outskirts of the small town. The dirt road gave way to asphalt, and the rolling hills opened into a charming main street. Her heart lifted as she took in the transformation. Greg had been right—there were big changes.

Five years ago, Duckinwilla Creek's shops had looked like relics of the last century—faded signs, peeling paint, and an air of quiet resignation. Now, the town seemed to hum with life. She widened her eyes, unable to believe the number of shoppers in the street, even this early in the day. Each side of the road was lined with parked cars.

As Charlotte cruised down the familiar main

street, nostalgia washed over her. The small cluster of businesses had been painted and refurbished but still retained their charm and quirky character. If anything, the charm had been enhanced.

She slowed as she passed Lucy-Lou's Hairdressing Salon, a cheerful shop front painted in soft pastel hues of pink and lavender. The scalloped awning added a touch of whimsy, and the bold, looping sign with 'Lucy-Lou's' scrawled in gold glitter paint sparkled in the sunlight. Inside, she caught a glimpse of Lucy-Lou herself, a petite woman with a bright red beehive, chatting animatedly as she trimmed a client's hair. Lucy-Lou was known for her retro style and infectious laughter that often spilled out onto the street.

Just next door, Jerry's Barber Shop stood in contrast, with a newly polished wooden exterior and red-and-white striped pole. The windows were filled with posters of classic cars and old rock bands, and the interior had always had an unmistakable masculine vibe, with dark leather chairs and a faint scent of cedar. Jerry, with his neatly trimmed grey moustache and suspenders, was busy chatting with a customer while wielding a pair of scissors. Charlotte had sat here in the school holidays when Papa had his hair cut.

Lucy-Lou and Jerry were a delightfully odd pair—married for decades but adamant about keeping their businesses and homes separate.

Further along, Charlotte passed the milk bar, a retro-looking shop with checkerboard tiles. She wondered if Con still ran it. When she was growing up, he'd run his milk bar through the day and played guitar in the local bowling club at night. The milk bar where she'd spent countless afternoons sharing hot chips and secrets with friends bore a fresh coat of paint but still had its fading Coca-Cola sign. It had been a favourite stop after coming home on the long bus ride from high school in Maryborough. Then she'd had a part-time job there the last two summers she was home.

She smiled, remembering the bus trips—how she'd tried to sit quietly and read, only to be drawn into the hijinks of her friends. Marley's sarcastic quips, Sabina's contagious laugh, and Jenny's endless curiosity about everything they passed along the way had made those journeys unforgettable.

Now, Marley was a high-flying lawyer in Perth. Sabina was pursuing her passion in an Adelaide art gallery, and Jenny had found her calling at a wildlife park in the Northern Territory. They'd all taken different paths, yet Charlotte knew their connection hadn't faded. Once she settled in France, she would email them, sharing the news that she, too, had finally achieved her dream. The thought made her happy, and she promised herself she wouldn't let too much time pass before she reached out to them.

Mr Elliott's butcher shop, once a tired brick building, now boasted a vintage-inspired façade with cream-coloured paint and a neat striped awning. A blackboard sign leaned against the wall, listing daily specials in elegant chalk script.

Next door, Mrs Boyd's haberdashery charmed with its display of colourful wares. Pots of silk flowers flanked the entrance, and hand-knitted jumpers in soft pastels swayed gently on a rack outside. Her eyes widened; if she was seeing correctly, there were fresh tulips for sale in jugs on a table near the step.

Further along, where there had once been a bakery, a small dress boutique filled the building.

The bakery had once been the busiest shop in the street, and she was surprised it had closed.

Even the Duckinwilla Hotel had undergone a transformation. Its weathered exterior was now a vision of French provincial charm, complete with shuttered windows and climbing vines. There was a new car park at the side, a clear sign that the pub was thriving.

Charlotte slowed, her eyes widening as she took it all in. Duckinwilla Creek had changed—and for the better. Perhaps Grandmère had had a say in the refurbishment; there was definitely a French feel to the town. Guilt niggled at Charlotte as she realised how long she'd stayed away. Five years was a long time to hold a grudge.

But it was the family store that stopped her heart. Gone was the cluttered, dimly lit shop of her father's era. The old store with the tables and chairs outside in their mishmash of timber laminated tops, with some timber, but mostly plastic chairs, the store that she'd loved.

She knew it had annoyed Grandmère, but Dad had had no thought of creating an ambience that was enticing to customers. He saw the store as a grocery and hardware store and had fought against the installation of the coffee shop at the front. Grandmère had won that argument. The interior had been dark and cluttered, but in its own way, it had held a timeless charm. There were few old stores like that left in the country these days.

In place of the family store stood an elegant establishment with The General Store spelled out in gold letters on a sleek black sign. It looked classy. The shopfront was a delightful hodgepodge of French-inspired charm, with crates of fresh produce arranged under the awning. Strings of garlic and onions hung from the rafters, and a penny-farthing bicycle leaned against the wall. Black wrought iron tables and chairs sat on the side of the two steps that led up into the interior of the store, and another half-dozen tables scattered along the footpath were covered with brightly coloured tablecloths. Baskets of colourful flowers hung from the awning over the footpath, and a jug of flowers sat on each table.

This was what Greg had been talking about. A flutter of warmth filled her as she imagined him walking into her family store.

Charlotte shook her head as she stared at the

new exterior. Grandmère had told her nothing of the refurbishment of the main street. Three of those tables had customers seated there even at this early hour. The enticing smell of freshly brewed coffee and baked goods drifted across to Charlotte and made her nose twitch.

Things had certainly changed. She walked up the steps and pushed open one of the double doors, and the bell tinkled above the door as it always had.

Her surprise deepened as she looked around; it was as though she was in a different place: bright lights, shiny cabinets, a new coffee machine, and aisles filled with crates of potatoes and onions gave it a welcoming and modern feel.

The store was now open and spacious, with a counter along the wall where the plumbing bits used to be. Her eyes tracked along to the side wall, where an upmarket delicatessen counter now filled the space. It was as though she had stepped into a French patisserie; it reminded her of the trendy delicatessens in Brisbane.

Even though it was only just after nine, the shop was full, and three women served behind the two counters and another one at the main cash register at the back of the store. That had always been there—well, the old register had been there, but now it was modernised with a white Square EFTPOS screen on a stand, sitting next to a jug of colourful flowers. Apart from that, there was nothing on the counter.

The counter was usually a mess of Dad's creation; it had been covered with receipts and dockets and invoice books, and half the time, a cup of cold instant coffee usually sat beside the register. Memories filtered down as Charlotte looked around. Dad had always refused to drink the brewed coffee from the machine.

Was he here?

She shook her head, unable to believe what she was seeing. There was no sign of him, and she wondered where he was. And, more to the point, how he'd ever agreed to these changes. The staff working seemed to be efficient, and the customers looked satisfied with their purchases. She didn't recognise a single person in the whole store.

She took a step further into the store and smiled when she saw Julien, who had stayed in touch regularly over the last five years, standing at the back of the store talking to Rowena Billings. She'd never been friends with Rowena even though they'd been in the same year at high school. She decided to wait until they finished their conversation, but her attention focused on them as Rowena's voice rose, and Julien took a step back. He held one hand up and shook his head.

'Obviously an unhappy customer,' she thought, as Rowena's whining voice drew attention, and heads began to turn.

'I'm not going to let this go, Julien,' she said loudly.

Charlotte could see the concern on her brother's face, and she decided to intervene.

She hurried past the stands of colourful tropical fruit and the hanging bunches of herbs and stepped around to the corner where bags of pasta lined the shelves.

'Julien,' she said quietly. The first time, he didn't hear her, so she took a step closer. 'Julien,' she repeated.

This time, his head lifted, and a strange expression crossed his face: discomfort, embarrassment, and then joy.

'Charlotte!' He stepped forward with both his hands outstretched, his voice a mix of happiness and surprise. 'When did you get here?

You must've left Brisbane very early. We weren't expecting you until the afternoon.'

'I got here last night,' she said, turning to be polite to Rowena, who was watching them with a scowl.

'Hello, Rowena.'

Rowena gave out a sound that was a cross between a grunt and a brief greeting, and Julien ignored her as he took both of Charlotte's hands. 'Come into the office with me, and we'll catch up.'

'Don't you ignore me, Julien! This will be going further. I'll be back later,' Rowena said, anger filling her voice.

Julien shrugged and led Charlotte to the office.

For a moment, Charlotte worried that Rowena was going to make a scene, and she glanced back at her. She was standing there with a malicious look on her face, staring after them.

'An unhappy customer?' Charlotte asked.

'Yes,' her brother said briefly, but he looked frazzled.

Julien opened the door to Dad's office, and again Charlotte was taken aback by the clear room—a desk, a phone, a filing cabinet, and a whiteboard filled with instructions: order coffee, cancel the last order, fix the roster.

She shook her head silently and then looked at her brother.

'Bit different to working on the farm, hey Charlie?'

'It certainly is,' she said. 'What happened?'

'Dad's decided to become a farmer these days. Cane's been getting a good price, and Oliver and Guy are still working on the farm. They do most of the heavy work, so when I came back from Sydney, he asked me whether I'd take over the store. And I did. You know how much I hated working on the farm.'

'You never mentioned you were in Sydney,' she said.

'I went down for a couple of years. I did a traineeship there at one of the top bakeries in the city.'

'So, all the time we were talking on the phone and by email, you weren't even at home. That explains why you didn't say much about the family. I thought it was because you thought I wouldn't want to hear anything.'

'I knew you had your demons to get over, sweetie, so I just wanted you to know that I'd always be here for you.'

'You didn't even tell me you had left and come home again,' she said.

'Well, there was no point when you didn't know that I'd gone in the first place.'

'Or that you had been studying!'

'I'm a qualified pastry chef now.' He looked sheepish and proud.

'How long have you been looking after the store?'

'About eighteen months,' he said. 'When Dad pulled the pin to go and work on the farm, I closed the shop for a week and had a massive clean-out. The community was up in arms because they had to travel to Maryborough for their groceries. I had a mate from Sydney who came up and did all the shop-fitting for me.'

'It's incredible. You're in charge of the store! I mean, Mum and Dad used to run this by themselves, and now you've got what? How many staff?'

'Eight different girls who come in and work, and one guy who does the alcohol side of things.'

'And what do you do? Everything?' she asked, raising her eyebrows.

'I bake. And I supervise,' Julien said simply.

'That was the only reason I went to Sydney. To learn the trade.'

'You're amazing, Julien Johnson, I can't believe what you've done.'

'We open longer hours too. At night now, we open from five till seven on Friday, Saturday, and Sunday. We're licensed now, and we serve pizza. The response has been amazing. People come out here from Maryborough just for the pizzas.'

Charlotte gestured outside. 'The store looks amazing, and I love the new name: The General Store. Great sign. Did you do all of that, or did you have help?'

Julien's face brightened. 'Emily looks after the accounts and orders.'

'Emily?'

'You'll meet her while you're home. She came back from Sydney with me. I moved out of home, and we've renovated the flat above the store. We live there.'

'Gosh, you're a dark horse. You've never mentioned you had a partner. I'll look forward to meeting her.'

Her brother pulled a face. 'I'm thinking about whether to invite her to this dinner

Grandmère's having. Maybe, maybe not.'

'Dinner? What dinner?' Charlotte rolled her eyes.

'Sorry, I thought you would have heard by now.'

'No, if Grandmère had mentioned a family dinner, I probably wouldn't have come home. And she would have known that, the shrewd old bird. When is it?'

'Tonight. I guess it can't hurt for Emily to see our family, warts and all, when we're together. So far, she's only met the family in bits and pieces. But the good news is that she and Grandmère have really hit it off.'

'Well, I'll come and meet Emily tonight here because I'm not going to any family dinner. I'll stay one night, and that's it. I can put up with being at home for one night.'

Julien went to speak and then stopped.

Charlotte's suspicions flared. 'What? What else is there?'

'Nothing. If you're leaving town, you don't need to know. Anyway, enough about me,' he said. 'Tell me how you're feeling about being back here.'

'Honestly? You haven't picked up on that

yet?' she asked.

'Yep, honestly.'

'Okay, I'm scared shitless. And I'm angry at myself for feeling that way because none of this stupid carry-on was my fault.'

'You look very composed and fresh. Love the dress.' He looked at her thoughtfully for a long moment before he spoke. 'Can I make you a coffee?'

'Yes, please.'

'Have you had breakfast?'

'No, I haven't.'

'Okay, I'll get Jenny to plate you a croissant. Do you want to sit out the front? I've got a couple of things to organise for the day, and then I'll come out and join you.'

'Sounds good. Sweet croissant too, please, not savoury.'

'You don't need to tell me that; I know your sweet tooth. Go and wait outside.' He reached out and put his arms around her. 'It's great to have you home, Charlie, even if it's only for a short while.'

Warmth flooded her, followed by regret for the loss of closeness the family once had.

After a moment, Charlotte stepped back,

blinking back the tears that had formed as her brother had held her. 'It's good to see you, too.'

She was aware that Julien was watching her as she walked through the store and went outside. There was no sign of the woman who had been talking to him before. She stepped outside, looked around, and headed for a vacant table past the barrels of polished, rosy apples and bright red tomatoes.

No sign of her out here either; she was curious about what had been going on. Julien had looked upset, but it was none of her business. She also sensed that he was holding back on something she should know, and that unsettled her. Her decision had been made; she'd see Mum and Dad at the farm, then go and visit Grandmère and Papa. Then she'd decide how long she was going to stay. Julien's welcome had been warm and genuine.

As she settled at the table and leaned back to look around, her phone buzzed on the table next to her. A horrid feeling crawled through her stomach again as she noticed that it was her mother calling. She hadn't spoken to her for several months.

For a moment, Charlotte considered

ignoring the call and waiting until she headed home after she'd had her coffee; she was in no rush, and their house was only three streets away.

Pulling a face, she pressed the answer button and sighed. 'Hi, Mum.' Charlotte forced brightness into her voice.

'Charlotte, where are you?' her mother said.

'I'm on my way,' she said.

'How far out are you?'

'An hour or so.' There was no need to tell her that she had stayed the night or that she was at the store. Mum would get upset that she hadn't come straight home first.

'So, you'll be here in an hour?'

'Yes, about that,' Charlotte said.

'We're home.'

'Okay. I'll see you soon.'

'Charlotte, hang on, wait. I've got a room ready for you at the farm. We're having dinner at Grandmère's new place tonight; everyone's coming to see you.'

Dread settled in Charlotte's stomach like a brick. 'At Grandmère's?'

'Yes, the farm's not good enough, apparently. Your father's mother has always thought she was better than I am.'

Charlotte closed her eyes. *Can I just turn around and leave now?*

'There's no need to have a dinner. I can just catch up with everyone when I'm here.'

'And how long will that be for?'

'I'm not sure yet.'

'No, I know you won't do that. Julien and your grandmother will be the only ones you talk to.'

For a moment, Charlotte wondered if Julien had called Mum, and she shook her head; he wouldn't have done that.

'We'll talk about it when I get there.'

'*No*, we're having dinner tonight. It's all organised.'

The dread in Charlotte's stomach deepened; it was just so typical of her mother. Everything was always so negative, and Lisette had inherited that trait. Charlotte, Julien, Oliver, Guy, and Amelia always looked on the positive side.

Poor Dad; no wonder he'd spent most of his time either buried in the store or now apparently out at the farm. The last thing he would want would be for Mum to be out there with him, criticising everything he did.

'Okay, Mum, I'll be out there in a while. I'll

see you then, and yes, all right, I will be at dinner tonight.' She disconnected before her mother could say anything more.

Why did I come home?

She needed a very strong coffee. Maybe even a shot of brandy in it.

No, she didn't need Dutch courage. She'd dig deep and get through this.

CHAPTER 5

Duckinwilla Creek

Charlotte slipped her phone into her handbag, switching it to silent with movements that had become a habit whenever her mother called. The morning sun warmed the wrought iron table as she tried to ground herself in the present moment. One day in Duckinwilla Creek. She could manage that.

The main street hummed with unfamiliar life—tourists with cameras and shopping bags, voices carrying the accent of the city. It was like watching a play being performed on a familiar stage with an entirely new cast.

Julien appeared with a massive latte and what looked like heaven on a plate—a croissant spilling with custard and fresh fruit. The sight of it momentarily pushed away the knot in her stomach.

'Oh, yum,' she said. 'Just what I need to cheer me up.'

'You need cheering up, do you?'

'No, just a figure of speech,' she said

quickly. 'I'm fine, Jules.' The lie came easily after five years of practice. 'I just can't get over the change in town.'

'Wait till you see the locals—what's left of them anyway.' He grinned. 'They only come out at dawn or dusk these days, like shy wildlife. Some reckon the tourism's got out of hand.'

'But surely it's good for business?'

'It is.' Something flickered across his face. 'Though not everyone's happy about the changes. Grandmère and I aren't exactly winning popularity contests.'

Ah. That explained the French provincial touches. Charlotte gestured at the wrought iron furniture and hanging baskets. 'Her design?'

'Got it in one.' He squeezed her hand. 'Anyway, the girls are busy inside. I'll have to go and help for a while. I'll see you tonight at Grandmère and Papa's.'

'Apparently everyone's been summoned.'

'Don't worry, Charlie. What you imagine is always worse than reality. We've got your back.'

'We?'

'Most of us.' The careful choice of words spoke volumes. 'And Grandmère, of course.'

Most, but not all. Not their parents, clearly.

And definitely not Lisette. As Julien went back into the store, her thoughts were sad.

Most of her siblings, and no mention of Mum or Dad. Lisette was the one she was dreading seeing because she didn't know whether she could keep her thoughts to herself. If she said what she was thinking, it could destroy her relationship with the family forever.

Before Charlotte could dwell on that thought, a familiar voice cut through the morning bustle.

'Charlotte?'

She turned, and her heart did a complicated little dance. Greg Barrett stood there, looking decidedly un-head-teacher-like in jeans and a faded T-shirt that showed off arms more suited to farm work than staff meetings.

'May I sit?' Greg Barrett said.

She nodded, hoping the heat creeping up her neck wasn't visible. 'What on earth are you doing here?'

'Visiting family.' His smile reached his eyes, crinkling the corners in a way she'd always found distracting during staff meetings.

'Well, wow, it's good to see you.'

'It'll be good to have a chat as normal

people,' he said. 'It's hard being a head teacher. I shouldn't say that, but it's true. You can't really socialise with staff when you're in charge, so you're better off keeping a professional distance. But I can chat with you now because you're not on staff anymore.'

Charlotte smiled. 'Yes, I thought it might be hard being in charge. They're a nice group of people, but there are definitely some strong opinions in the staff room.'

'And we'll leave it at that,' Greg said. 'School holidays and you're not going back—when did you arrive?'

'Last night.' She pulled a face. 'For the obligatory family catch-up before I head overseas. What about you? I thought you were going to Dunmora.'

'Oh, I'll get there,' he said with a shrug. 'I took a few detours sightseeing.'

'You don't sound like you're in a hurry to get home.'

'It's always difficult going back home when you don't meet family expectations.'

'Tell me about it.' The words slipped out before she could catch them. 'So you're off to France for a holiday?' she said, still unable to believe Greg was here.

'I am. When I drove away from school the other day, I took all of my things with me. Can I be honest with you? Promise you won't say anything to the others?'

'I won't. You can trust me.'

'I'm thinking about not going back to the school,' he admitted. 'I've spoken to the principal, and he's keeping the job open for me for two weeks while I decide.'

'That really surprises me, Greg. You always seemed happy there.'

'It's a job,' he said with a shrug. 'It pays the bills. Teaching wasn't really a calling for me.'

'But you've done so well—you're a head teacher at your age!'

'I'm not that young,' he chuckled. 'It's given me flexibility to travel, but now I need to figure out if I want to keep going for another year.'

'So, when do you leave for France?'

'In a week. I thought I'd spend a week with the olds first.'

'Me too,' she said. 'I'm here for at least one night. Maybe more. Family's always—interesting.'

'Sounds like we both have stories to tell.'

His eyes met hers. 'Save them for that coffee in France?'

'Or you could join me now?' The invitation surprised her even as she made it. 'My brother makes a mean coffee.'

His eyes crinkled at the corners as he looked at her. 'I'd love to. I'll go and order now. Thanks, Charlotte.' Greg's grin widened as he stood and disappeared inside. Charlotte reached for her fork and cut the croissant into three pieces. She couldn't resist. She brought a creamy, light piece to her mouth and closed her eyes.

Superb.

Duckinwilla Creek did have some redeeming qualities.

While she waited for Greg, she turned her attention to the growing crowds on the main street, still fascinated by the changes in the town and the number of unfamiliar faces.

Until she noticed the young woman standing at the edge of the footpath.

Charlotte rolled her eyes, but her stomach clenched, and her breathing quickened.

CHAPTER 6

Duckinwilla Main Street

'Home to show us how well you've done, are you?' Her sister, Lisette, stood there glaring at her.

For a moment, the dread in Charlotte's stomach was physical, sitting there like a hard ball. She swallowed, terrified that she was going to bring up the croissant she had just eaten.

Then common sense prevailed. If Lisette wanted a confrontation, this wasn't the right place for it. Besides, Greg would be back outside any moment, and she didn't want him to see what trouble she'd apparently caused in the family.

Charlotte kept her voice even. 'Hello, Lisette. How are you? Not happy, I see.'

'What do you care? I never want to speak to you again.'

'You're the one who started this conversation.' She forced a smile to her face.

'Why are you back here?'

'To see my family.'

'Well, I don't want to see you. None of them

realise what you're like.' Lisette's face was red, and her mouth was pursed.

'You know what?' Charlotte said softly, aware of the curious looks from the people at the table beside her. 'I let what you did worry me for a long time, but now I've realised that, in the scheme of life with tragedies and sadness, what happened doesn't matter. I've forgiven you,' Charlotte said.

Lisette's face went bright red. '*You've* forgiven me? How dare you say that!'

More heads began to turn at the nearby tables. Charlotte lifted her napkin and dabbed at her mouth to keep her composure.

'This isn't the place to have this conversation,' she said calmly. 'Perhaps we can continue it tonight. Shall we meet a little earlier? Before we go to Grandmère's?'

'No. I don't even know if I'm going. If you're going to be there, I don't want to be. I couldn't eat anything, so there's no point.'

Charlotte shrugged. 'Suit yourself. But, as I said, I'm not having this conversation here. You've always liked the attention. Remember I always said you should go into acting? Still a drama queen, I see.'

Lisette glared at her, then turned and strode away. She disappeared around the pub corner.

By the time Greg came back out, Charlotte had calmed down and smiled at him when he sat down. She looked up as Julien placed a coffee and another croissant in front of Greg.

'I didn't realise you were with Charlotte.'

'Julien. This is my friend, Greg. We worked at the same school together in Brisbane, and it's a pure coincidence that we happen to be here at the same time. We just bumped into each other.'

'A cosy coincidence.' Julien winked at her, and the heat flew up her neck again.

'Julien, don't you start.'

'I won't, Charlie. You know I'm only teasing you. Hi, Greg. Good to meet you.'

Greg smiled at him. 'Ditto. Love the store, and this croissant looks amazing.'

'It is,' Charlotte said. 'It's certainly cheered me up.'

Julien flashed her an enigmatic look. 'Lisette? I saw her walking away when I brought the coffee out to the table near the door.'

Charlotte nodded.

Her brother shook his head as he headed back to the door. 'I'll get you another one.'

'I like Charlie. Suits you.'

'Julien has always called me that. To the rest of the family, I'm Charlotte.'

'You need cheering up?' Greg asked.

'No, all good,' she said. 'I'm fine, but thanks, Greg.' Charlotte reached for her coffee, but it spilled into the saucer as her hand shook.

Quickly, Greg grabbed a napkin from the middle of the table and dabbed at the spill. 'You didn't burn yourself, did you?'

Charlotte shook her head. 'No, sorry. I'm fine, just clumsy.'

'Are you okay?'

'Yeah, I'm okay. Just my thoughts were elsewhere.'

'I hope they're happy thoughts.'

'I wish,' Charlotte said.

'Now,' he said, 'tell me your travel itinerary. You'll be starting pretty early in January, I guess, with the school year?'

'Actually, no. I have a couple of weeks to travel because the person I'm replacing is going on maternity leave. She'll work for the first two weeks, then stay the third week to show me the ropes. I'll take over around early February.'

'Sounds good.'

'Yeah, and I figured being in France would give me a real opportunity to immerse myself in the language. What about you? Where are you going?'

'Well, I decided not to start in Paris. I'm flying into the *Côte d'Azur*, hiring a car, and making my way through the countryside. My sister lives in a little village near Avignon. Beaune.'

'Really? That's where my grandmother came from,' she said.

'So, you'll visit there, I guess?'

'For sure. Like you, I'm flying to Nice. I figured I'd explore the south of France before heading to Lyon. But, unlike you, I'm not driving. I'm bad enough on Australian roads, let alone driving on the wrong side at those speeds.'

'How will you get around?'

'I'll bus and train it. My schedule is pretty flexible.'

'Once I get the car, I'm free. We should exchange numbers, and if you're stuck over there, please don't hesitate to call. I could take you sightseeing.'

'That's very kind of you, Greg.'

'It'd be nice to have company before I meet

up with my sister. Give it some thought.'

'I will.'

It was hard to reconcile this friendly, cheerful man with the head teacher, who had kept to himself, only speaking to staff during meetings.

Maybe he was unhappy, and no one noticed.

Greg interrupted her thoughts. 'We all tend to get caught up in our own world, don't we?'

'Yes, even at school,' she agreed.

'And families,' he said. 'But I'm going to do my duty, try to get back in Dad's will.' He chuckled. 'Dad always joked about me being in there in pencil. Don't get me wrong; I do love my parents.'

Charlotte smiled. It was nice to hear a man say that.

'But they can make it very hard at times. I never measured up.'

'What do they do?'

'They live on a cane farm, but Dad has a manager who looks after the day-to-day operations. Dad's a lawyer, and his office is in Maryborough. He expected me to follow him into law.'

'But you wanted to teach,' she said.

'Yes, I thought I did. But after eight years of it, I think Dad might've been right. Maybe I should have done law.'

'Well, you've got a logical mind. I appreciated your logic as head teacher—your instructions and programs were clear and easy to follow.'

'Teaching didn't give me what I expected,' he admitted.

They shared a look of understanding.

'I think part of it was I'd loved school so much as a student, and I wanted to be a part of that, but it's very different when you're teaching children or teenagers, I suppose, and dealing with staff—many of whom don't want to be there either. It wasn't a very pleasant place to be, and the expectations of the department now, with outcomes and data, make the role of the executive very difficult.'

'You never had any aspirations to go higher?'

'Hell no. I think my biggest aspiration these days is to get out of there.'

'I guess you've answered your own question, then—that you had two weeks to make up your mind?'

Greg shrugged and nodded. 'I think I have.'

'You'll be missed.'

'So will you.'

'I guess we're a pair,' she said, looking searchingly. 'Looking for our place in life and what we really want to do.' She looked past him and said half to herself, 'and where we want to do it.'

'Without family expectations,' he said.

The conversation between Charlotte and Greg was animated as they discovered they had more in common than coming from the local area.

'You know, we've wasted the last two years,' she said. 'We could've known about each other earlier.' She glanced at her watch. 'I'm going to have to be rude and go soon, though. My parents are expecting me out at the farm around eleven.'

She pushed her plate in front of her and placed her cup and saucer on it. Greg did the same, nodding, but there was not a crumb left on either plate. 'I can't believe I ate two of those croissants.'

'They were only small. I'm going to buy some to take home,' Greg said.

He's a good chef, isn't he?'

'Julien, your brother—he is a chef?'

'Yes. A pastry chef. He's been working in Sydney for a couple of years, apparently, and he came home to take over the family store. I don't know all the details, but I guess I'll find them out tonight at dinner.'

'I can see you're not looking forward to that,' Greg said.

'I'm certainly not.'

He stood, came around, and held her chair as she stood. She smiled at his lovely manners.

'Thank you,' she said.

'It's been fabulous to catch up. Do you still have the same number you had at school, or is that your work mobile?'

'No, same number,' she said.

'Would you mind if I gave you a call in the next week or so? Maybe we could spend a day together, go for a drive, or have a picnic?'

'Escape from your family?' she said with a grin.

'Respite from yours?' he replied.

'Yes, that would be lovely,' she said. 'I'm not sure how long I'll stay, but if things get too bad, I'll just pack up and go back to Brisbane.'

'Maybe a bit of different company in the middle of your visit will make it easier.'

'I'll look forward to it,' she said.

'You know what?' he said. 'So will I.'

'Greg, please call me.'

'I promise. I'll text you when I go back to the car, and if you need rescuing earlier, give me a call.'

The morning sun warmed Charlotte's face as she watched Greg walk away, a spring in his step she'd never seen during their school days. Something had shifted between them over coffee and croissants—the strict head teacher replaced by a man questioning his own path just as much as she was questioning hers.

'Give me a call if you need rescuing,' he'd said, and she knew he meant it.

She might take him up on that sooner than expected, especially after Lisette's performance. Her sister's bitter words still echoed: "None of them realise what you're like." The accusation carried five years of festering resentment.

CHAPTER 7

The family farm

As Charlotte strolled back to her car, she let the town's transformation distract her from darker thoughts. The town had a lively feel now, and she enjoyed the buzz of tourists and cheerful chatter. She wasn't in a rush to get to the farm; her mother would be busy in the kitchen, and her father would be out in the cane fields with her brothers. It was easier to avoid one-on-one conversations with her mother, who would dive straight into the heavy stuff. If Lisette's behaviour was anything to go by, nothing had changed. If she left tomorrow, she'd have to ring Greg and tell him she was going back to Brisbane. She didn't want him to think she was giving him the flick.

The new dress boutique caught her eye—designer labels that would have been unthinkable in the old Duckinwilla CreekCharlotte browsed through racks of clothing, pulling out a white jumper and holding it against herself in the mirror. Out of the corner of her eye, she noticed a woman watching her; it was Rowena Billings.

'That's a pretty dress,' Charlotte said, gesturing to Rowena's selection.

'Yes, I need some maternity dresses.' Rowena's tone was carefully neutral, but something in her expression made Charlotte's instincts prickle.

'Congratulations,' she managed, but as she moved left, snippets of a hushed conversation reached her ears.

'He wouldn't talk to me,' Rowena bitterly.

Another voice that sounded suspiciously like Lisette's answered. 'That's awful. What are you going to do?'

Charlotte's stomach clenched. What new drama was brewing in Duckinwilla Creek?

The drive to the farm was pleasant. Charlotte opened a Spotify calm music selection on her phone, and Bluetoothed it to the car's audio system. She repeated an affirmation she kept pinned to her fridge in Brisbane. By the time she reached the dirt road leading to the farmhouse, her nerves had settled.

A little.

The family farm stretched out before her as Charlotte pulled up to the shed, work utes lined up like sentries by the creek. The smell of roasting meat drifted from the house, along with memories she wasn't ready to face.

After reapplying her lipstick and smoothing her hair, she made her way to the house. She hesitated at the front door, debating whether to knock or just walk in. Five years had turned her into a stranger in her childhood home. Instead, she circled to the back, where her mother would see her from the kitchen window.

The garden had gone wild, flowering shrubs tangled with long grass. Her mother had always kept it neat when they were kids, worried about snakes. But there were no small children here now. So much had changed, and she knew so little about her siblings' lives.

'You there, Mum?'

The house was quiet, but she spotted her parents by the shed, heads close in conversation. For a moment, she watched them—her father greyer she remembered, her mother's shoulders stiff with tension.

'Hey, Mum, Dad!'

They jumped apart like guilty teenagers. Her father managed a smile as Charlotte hugged him, feeling him stiffen before relaxing slightly. Her mother's greeting was frost-edged.

'It's been a long time, Charlotte.'

'Five years,' her father muttered, raising an eyebrow.

'Please don't start.' Charlotte fought to keep her voice steady. 'I want this to be a pleasant visit.'

'Not much chance of that,' her mother muttered under her breath.

Charlotte swallowed the lump forming in her throat. 'Well, I'm determined to enjoy seeing everyone,' she said brightly.

Even if they don't make it easy.

'Put the kettle on, love. There's no point starting an argument,' Dad said, running a hand through his hair.

Dad squeezed her hand as they walked to the house, the gesture worth more than words. Charlotte stared at him as Mum headed up the back steps. Dad had lost weight.

'Are you well, Dad?' she asked as he walked beside her.

'I'm okay. It's been a big harvesting season. It's good to see you home, Charlotte.'

She blinked back tears as Dad held the screen door open for her.

Inside, her mother's ramrod-straight back at the sink spoke volumes. It wouldn't take much more for her just to get in the car and go. She fought the tears that were threatening. How did her life come to this?

And why did I come home?

Swallowing hard, she put a chirpy note into her voice. 'I was really surprised when I drove through town. It's really nice, and I was even more surprised when I went to the store and saw how different it looked. And then I found Julien there.'

'Is that where you've been?' Mum said.

'Yes, I had a quick cup of coffee there, and I met a friend who happened to be in town. That's what delayed me.'

'Fair enough.' Her mother accepted her excuse. 'Grab the cups for me, would you please, Charlotte? If you remember where they are?'

Charlotte forced a smile to her face. 'I do remember where they are. I'm surprised you came to work on the farm, Dad. I thought the boys were going to do it.'

'Guy and Oliver do the heavy stuff. Your father had a bit of a health scare last year, and the stress of running the store for the last two years was too much for him.'

'A health scare? No one told me.'

'Would you have been interested?' Mum said.

'Mum, don't be unfair. Of course I would've been interested.' Charlotte swallowed again and folded her arms. 'Look, can we just move past all of this anger? I'm home. It's lovely to see you, and I'd like to have a happy time here with you all before I head to France. Is that too much to ask?' To her dismay, her voice broke on the last words.

Dad reached for her hand again, and this time, she was unable to catch that single tear that spilled down her cheek.

'Of course we can. Now tell us about what you've been doing at the school in Brisbane.' He pulled out a chair for her to sit on. 'Have you been teaching French?'

'I have, and doing that has really helped me with the language, I think. Grandmère is going to be very pleased, although there's nothing like being immersed in the language of the country. I'm looking forward to going to France and learning some more.'

'Do you like being a teacher?' Mum's

contribution to the conversation was made in a slightly disapproving tone.

'I do, and I enjoyed working with the girls in the language department. It was a very good school.'

'Then why are you leaving?'

'I want to experience new things. Spend some time in France, see some of Europe.'

'Duckinwilla Creek is enough for the rest of our kids,' Mum said.

'Julien went to Sydney. He told me he did his pastry chef training there.'

'He did. He's very good,' Mum said. 'But he came home and—'

Dad interrupted, 'And as much as I hate to say it, he has done a great job at the store. I could never have got myself organised to do that.'

Mum smiled for the first time. 'And Emily is a lovely young woman. Did you meet her?'

'No, I'm looking forward to it. I believe Julien is thinking about bringing her to dinner tonight.'

'I hope so. I'll give her a call and make sure she comes. Is that alright with you, Charlotte?' Every word niggled.

'Of course it is. Tell me about the others.

Julien said Oliver and Guy are working on the farm. I saw a few utes when I drove past the shed earlier.' She stumbled over her words as she realised what she had said.

'Earlier?' Mum looked at her. 'What were you doing out this way earlier? Why didn't you stop?'

'I just went for a bit of a drive. I went to town.'

'It's a strange way to come in from Brisbane.'

Charlotte laughed it off. There was no way that her mother was going to find out she'd spent the night at *Maison de Rêve*. 'I just wanted to see the district again. It's very beautiful. It looks like you've had a lot of rain, have you, Dad?'

'Yes, it's been a good season, and the cattle are going well too.'

Charlotte swallowed. 'And what about the girls? What are Lisette and Amelia up to?'

'Have you not been talking to them recently?'

'I saw Lisette briefly in town, but we didn't talk.' *Civilly, anyway.* 'I know Amelia was enrolling in the preschool course after school. Has she finished it?'

Mum's chest puffed out with pride. 'Not only has she finished it, but she got a job for next year at the kindergarten in town.'

'Oh, that's wonderful. I can imagine her doing that.'

'She's doing very well,' Dad said.

'And Lisette?'

'She works part-time in the bistro at the pub,' Mum said, lifting her chin. 'We couldn't afford to send her to uni.'

There was a sting in her words, but Charlotte didn't remind her mother that she had put herself through university. Nothing was stopping Lisette from doing the same.

And now for the elephant in the room, Charlotte thought. She took a deep breath and tried to speak calmly.

'And Brett?'

Her mother's expression held disbelief that Charlotte had raised him. 'I'm sure she'll tell you tonight.'

Charlotte didn't miss the glance her parents exchanged. 'So, what time tonight?' she asked.

'Are you going over to your grandmother's this afternoon, or do you want to get ready here?'

'I'll go after I finish my cup of tea.' The cup

of tea that Mum still hadn't made. 'In fact, don't worry about one for me. I'll head over there now and see if I can help.'

'Your grandmother will be holding court in the kitchen, giving poor Mrs Hyslop a hard time.'

'It will be good to see everyone,' Charlotte said, ignoring the barb directed at Grandmère.

She was just about out of conversation, and that made her so sad. Five years since she had been home, and the conversation with her parents felt shallow.

No questions about her life, whether she'd met anyone, whether she was happy. She felt abandoned; she shouldn't have come home.

That feeling of abandonment had given her some issues over the first couple of years she'd been away. Her counsellor had explained that was why she felt disconnected, as though she couldn't belong anywhere. It had even taken six months before she'd succumbed to Rosie and Mandy's friendship overtures at Helen's Creek High School.

Her father must have picked up her sadness. 'Stay and have a cuppa, love. You've only just got here.'

Mum went over to fill the teapot. 'Do you want a biscuit, or did Julien feed you at the store?'

'A biscuit would be nice, thank you.' At least if she were chewing, she wouldn't have to talk. Charlotte could feel herself spiralling down, not the depression that had led her to see the counsellor in her first year at university, and he'd told her she was suffering from depression. The feeling that was bubbling up into her throat was exactly the way she'd felt that year.

Coming home was a huge mistake. She should have stayed in Brisbane and got on that plane to France and forgotten about her family.

When Mum's back was turned, Dad reached over and took her hand again. He squeezed it gently and looked at her, shaking his head slightly.

Charlotte could have sworn his eyes were brimming with tears.

CHAPTER 8

Her grandparents' house

The sugarcane fields blurred past Charlotte's window, their waving mauve flower fronds a backdrop she'd once loved but now barely registered. Tears pricked at her eyes as she drove away from her parents' farm, the morning's stilted conversation replaying in her mind. The vibrant greens and the golden sun cast a warm glow over the land, but she felt none of its warmth.

Her heart closed as the conversation—or lack thereof—with her parents stayed with her; why did everyone hate her so much? Was she so unworthy? She had tried so hard to be a good child and a good daughter. As she navigated the winding road, memories of happier times, interspersed with moments of tension, filled her thoughts.

When she finally arrived at Grandmère and Papa's new house, she barely had time to catch her breath before stepping out of the car.

As she approached the entrance, Charlotte

caught sight of Papa through the window. It felt like walking into a haven, a sanctuary that promised acceptance. Her distress lifted slightly; she could always rely on her grandparents.

The door swung open, and Papa stood there, his face lighting up with joy. 'Charlotte, my dear!' he called, his arms wide open. Before she could even think, she felt herself enveloped in a warm embrace. The smell of his cologne, coupled with a hint of lavender from the garden, wrapped around her like a comforting blanket. At that moment, all her worries began to subside.

'Papa,' she whispered, the word barely escaping her lips through the lump in her throat.

He stepped back slightly, his hands still resting on her shoulders as he studied her face. 'You're here now, *ma chérie*,' he said softly, his voice soothing. 'Come inside.'

As he ushered her in, Charlotte could barely focus on her surroundings. The foyer faded into the background as her emotions threatened to overwhelm her. She felt her knees weaken, and before she could centre herself, she collapsed into his embrace again, tears spilling down her cheeks.

'Oh, my sweet girl, what's wrong?' Papa

murmured; his voice was filled with concern. The genuine love in his eyes brought more tears.

Charlotte, barely able to speak, clung to him. The pain, the isolation, and the struggles she had faced over five years bubbled to the surface. Held in the warmth of her grandfather's embrace, she slowly calmed.

She wiped her eyes. 'I'm sorry, Papa. It was just so lovely to see you that I couldn't hold my tears back. I know how welcome I am here.' She gestured around. 'I adore your new house.'

'I guess your welcome at the farm wasn't very warm?' Grandmère stood in the doorway watching them. She held out her hand and led Charlotte to the couch. 'It is wonderful to see you, my sweet Charlotte. It's been too long. We have been guilty of neglecting you, too.'

Charlotte knew that Grandmère would not criticise Mum directly, but they had never had a close relationship. On the other hand, Mum took every opportunity to criticise Grandmère; she had never been happy with the time Charlotte had spent there. Lisette had quickly become Mum's favourite daughter, and even though it had made her sad, Charlotte had accepted the way things were. She often wondered what

Lisette had said to her parents for them to be so distant when she moved to Brisbane.

Charlotte shook her head as she sat on the plush couch adorned with floral patterns; Grandmère looked at her with a softness that belied her backbone of steel. 'My dear, we've missed you immensely,' she began, her voice gentle yet unwavering. 'Where are you staying? At the farm? You are most welcome to stay here if you would like some space.'

'I stayed at *Maison de Rêve* last night. I hope that was all right?'

'Of course it was.' Grandmère sat forward and looked at her intently.

Charlotte took a deep breath, the warmth of their welcome clashing with the coldness of her mother's. 'I just . . . I need to go back to Brisbane sooner. I can't stay here and fix the past. I thought I could. It's just too hard when I don't know what I'm supposed to have done.'

Papa leaned forward, his expression earnest. 'But Charlotte, we want you to stay. We all do. Tonight's dinner is a chance to confront what has happened finally. You can't run away from that.'

'What's done is done,' Charlotte murmured, shaking her head. 'There's no point in bringing it all up again. I don't want to relive it. I don't think I'm strong enough.'

'Of course you are, dear,' Grandmère interjected, her voice holding a firm but loving tone. 'It's time for the truth to come out. It is what I want for you. And Papa does, too. That way, you can go off to France and let all the sad memories go. Wait until I see your father. He will get a piece of my mind.'

'Dad was good.' A lump formed in her throat. 'You don't understand . . .' she began, her voice faltering.

'We do,' Papa said softly. 'We've witnessed the behaviour since you left.'

'Perhaps it was foolish to flee as you did,' Grandmère said. 'There have been so many stories; I don't think anyone knows the truth anymore. Some of our family has turned against you without knowing the truth.'

'What do you mean? What happened?' Charlotte asked, her heart racing.

Grandmère exchanged a glance with Papa, a silent understanding passing between them before she spoke. 'We found out from a neighbour about Lisette and Brett. Your grandfather had a conversation with them when they were out one day in town, unbeknownst to you. It was clear they'd been seeing each other behind your back for quite a while.'

'For how long?' Charlotte asked.

'A few months,' Grandmère said

'But Lisette would have only been fifteen then.'

Papa intervened. 'I spoke to your father about Lisette being underage, but I was told in no uncertain terms to mind my own business.'

'We tried to tell your parents that it had happened behind your back—' Grandmère hesitated—'but Lisette had already poisoned their minds against you.'

Charlotte's chest tightened. 'What do you mean poisoned?'

'Your sister has a way with words, my dear,' Papa explained gently. 'Your grandmother won't say it, but I will, so please forgive me. Your sister has a lot of your mother's traits.'

Charlotte frowned. 'I know she's always been the favourite.'

Papa reached out and took her hand. 'She painted you as the villain, saying you were cruel to Brett, that you thought you were better than him. Your mother believed her, and the lies got bigger with each retelling of Lisette's interpretation of what happened.'

'You know Lisette can be very, shall we say, persuasive.'

Charlotte's chest tightened as the pieces fell into place. Her little sister's talent for twisting truth, their mother's eagerness to believe the worst of her eldest daughter. The web of lies that had driven her from home five years ago.

'That is a polite way of describing what she does.' Charlotte pulled a face. 'I think she's stirring up trouble for Julien now.'

She is very much like Papa's mother; God rest her soul. She focuses on the negatives, and the truth gets distorted in any way that can make her look better. It is the only way she can feel good about herself. It is quite sad.' Grandmère reached over and took Charlotte's hands. 'But you, darling girl, are strong. You have completed your studies, you have worked in a good school, and now you have the wonderful opportunity to live in France. If I were younger, I would come with you!'

Charlotte felt something unfurl in her chest—not quite hope, but maybe its cousin. 'I still don't want to face everyone tonight.'

'You must. The truth will be told, and you can go overseas without the burden you have been carrying since you left here.'

Charlotte closed her eyes, remembering that day—seeing Brett kiss Lisette, the fight that followed, the way her world had shattered. 'I didn't think anyone would believe me. I was just so hurt. But why did they side with her? I thought they knew me, knew who I was. And I thought I knew my sister.'

'They didn't see everything,' Grandmère said, her eyes glistening with empathy. 'You became a scapegoat for Lisette's actions, and it wasn't fair to you. Sometimes the truth gets buried under lies and clever manipulation.'

'So, you knew?' Charlotte asked, a mix of disbelief and gratitude filling her heart.

'We knew,' Papa affirmed. 'But we were helpless against Lisette's influence. She spun that delicate web, and your parents became entrapped in it—just like you were. Oliver, Guy and Amelia stayed out of it.'

'And Julien?'

'He always believed in you.'

Something sparked in Charlotte's chest—not quite anger, not quite determination, but maybe both. 'Why should I face them again?'

'Because you deserve to reclaim your place in this family.' Grandmère's voice was fierce with love. 'Tonight's dinner will be the first step in healing. If you stay, you can finally express how you truly feel. It won't be easy, but it's necessary.'

Charlotte closed her eyes, feeling the warmth and love radiating from her grandparents. Something flickered in her chest—strength.

I can do this. Maybe it was time to stop running.

'Will you stay here tonight?' Papa asked gently.

'Would you mind terribly if I went back to *Maison de Rêve,* ?'

'Wherever you feel comfortable, *ma chérie.* As long as you come to dinner.'

Charlotte thought for a long minute, and then she smiled at her grandparents. 'Okay,' she said softly, 'I'll stay for dinner. I owe it to myself to face them—and to confront Lisette. But . . . could I bring a guest?'

She smiled at the surprise on their faces. It actually mirrored the surprise that she was feeling at the random decision to invite Greg to dinner. Grandmère's eyebrows rose with elegant surprise. 'A guest?'

'Someone I worked with in Brisbane.' Heat crept up Charlotte's neck. 'He's actually from around here—Greg Barrett. His family has the cane farm at Dunmora.'

'Ah, the Barretts.' Papa nodded approvingly. 'Good people.'

'He's visiting his family too,' Charlotte added quickly. 'We bumped into each other at the store this morning.'

A knowing smile played at the corners of Grandmère's mouth. 'The head teacher you mentioned in your calls? The one who was always so . . . professional?'

Charlotte felt her cheeks warm. Trust Grandmère to remember every detail she'd let slip over the years. 'He's different outside of school. More relaxed.'

'I'm sure he is.' Grandmère's eyes sparkled. 'And of course he's welcome. The more witnesses to tonight's truth-telling, the better.'

'I haven't asked him yet,' Charlotte cautioned. 'He might not want to get involved in family drama.'

'*Ma chérie*,' Grandmère said softly, 'a man who follows you from Brisbane to Duckinwilla Creek—even by coincidence—might be willing to face more than you think.'

Charlotte's heart did a little skip. She pulled out her phone, and Greg's number was already appearing on the screen. Sometimes, the scariest decisions were the ones that felt most right.

CHAPTER 9

Dunmora

Contentment hummed through Greg as he drove toward Dunmora, the memory of Charlotte's smile warming him more than the Queensland sun. She'd looked different from the quiet teacher he knew—radiant in her yellow dress, red lipstick highlighting a smile that reached her eyes. He caught himself grinning as he turned up the radio, singing along without a care in the world.

He'd detoured to Duckinwilla Creek hoping to run into Charlotte, though he'd never admit it. Now, with the promise of dinner ahead, even the dreaded homecoming felt lighter.

The Barrett family home stood silent when he arrived, its familiar rooms feeling oddly distant. Memories echoed off the walls—childhood laughter, heated discussions about his future, the weight of expectations he'd spent years trying to escape. Greg sank onto the couch, pulling out his phone for distraction.

He decided he'd call Charlotte earlier than midweek. The thought of spending time with her in France cheered him up, too, and he pushed aside the unease about meeting his parents—a summons he wasn't particularly looking forward to. At least he'd have some time with Mum before his father got home from the office.

Greg sat on the couch in his parents' living room, glancing around the familiar space that felt oddly distant as he waited for them to return. Memories echoed off the walls—childhood laughter, heated discussions about his future, the weight of expectations he'd spent years trying to escape. Greg sank onto the couch, pulling out his phone for distraction. The small screen lit up, revealing Charlotte's name, and he quickly pressed the call button.

'Hey, Charlotte,' he said, trying to sound upbeat, aware of how much he wanted to ease whatever tension she was under.

'Hi, Greg. How are you?' she replied, attempting to sound cheerful, but he could hear the underlying strain.

'So-so. No one was home,' he admitted, disappointment creeping into his tone. 'I let myself in, but I feel like a stranger in my family home.'

The warmth in her voice made him smile. 'I completely understand. It's been complicated here, too. I'm really glad you called. I was about to phone you myself.'

'For a chat?' He tried not to sound too hopeful.

'Actually' she hesitated, 'would you consider being my support person at a family dinner tonight? It's complicated, but having you there would mean a lot.'

Greg's pulse quickened. 'I'd be honoured to be your support person.'

Her laugh came through the line, warm and genuine. 'It's weird asking you, but I could really use the backup.'

'You know,' he said softly, surprising himself with his honesty, 'I've been thinking about you since I left the store.'

Her breath caught. 'That's really . . . nice. Unexpected, but nice.'

'And I am free. My parents have plans. I called Mum to see where they were. They're on their way home now,' he answered, excitement sparking at the possibility of making plans with Charlotte.

'It's strange to think about having you there, but it might help me keep my head above water.'

'So, it's a date then? I'll bring a bottle of something nice,' he suggested, confidence rising.

'Sounds good.'

'Are you staying there?' he asked, curious about her plans.

'No, I'm back at *Maison de Rêve*, ,' she answered.

'Can I pick you up?' he offered, eager to make things easier for her.

She gave him directions to the house, and as he wrote them down, a flutter of excitement started to dance in his stomach. This felt like more than just a simple dinner; it was a step closer to the connection he'd been hoping for since they'd crossed paths.

Greg's parents arrived home about half an hour before he planned to leave to pick Charlotte up. The welcome was warmer than he had expected. Dad was particularly chatty, and Mum held him close.

'I'm so sorry we have to go out tonight,' she said. 'It's a function we can't get out of. I'm on the committee.'

'It's okay, Mum. As it turns out, I'm going out too.'

'Excellent. Tell me more about it shortly. Your father and I have to go and get ready. We'll have a quick sherry with you before we leave.'

Greg was ready to leave and was sitting in the living room when his father walked out wearing a tuxedo.

'You look very swish tonight, Dad.'

'Yes, your mother has organised some fancy do for Rotary. I've got to look the part. I'd rather stay home and watch the cricket, though.'

Greg smiled.

'Where are you going, son?' His father crossed to the bar and held up a decanter of whisky.

'Just a small one, thanks,' he said. 'A friend of mine has asked me to go to her family's house for dinner tonight over at Duckinwilla Creek.'

'I didn't realise you knew anyone over there.'

'It's actually someone I've been working with for the past couple of years.'

His father's eyebrows rose. 'A romance? Is that why you've come back home?'

'No, no, it's the first social occasion I've

spent with Charlotte—her family owns a cane farm over in the valley.'

'What's her last name?'

'Johnson.'

'I think I know her dad; he goes to the cane farmer meetings. Hugo Johnson?'

'I'm not sure; I haven't met him. I've met her brother, Julien.'

'Yes, that's the family. Julien used to come to the meetings with him, but I believe he's working at their store in town now.'

'Yes, that's right. Nice bloke.'

'They're a decent family; they've been in the district for many years.'

His father sat down and looked at the floor, and Greg sensed there was something on his mind.

'Is there something wrong, Dad?'

'Yes. I've been tough on you the last few years, and I'm sorry. You made your choice of teaching, and you've done very well in the short time that you've been doing it. I just want you to know I'm proud of you, mate.'

Greg's eyes widened. This was totally out of character for his usually quiet father.

'Thank you, Dad. I really appreciate that.

You don't know how much it means to me. But you know, I've been thinking; you may have been right.'

'Right? In what way?'

'I'll tell you now. I'm putting in my notice at Helen's Creek High. I'm thinking about going back to uni.'

'Can you afford to do that without working?'

'Yes, I've saved over the last few years, and I think it's time to make a change.'

'And what will you be studying?'

Greg sat back and watched his father as he answered. 'What would you say if I said law?'

His father sat up straight and stared back at him. 'Law? I didn't think you were interested in it.'

'I think I had to find my own way to come to it myself. If you're happy to have me working with you in a couple of years, I'd be happy to be part of the firm.'

His father stood up and walked over, grasping his shoulder. 'You don't know how happy you've made me, Greg. Don't get me wrong; you made your own choice, and it was difficult, but I've come to accept it. Even so, I have to accept you're a grown man and that it's your life. But, mate, you've made my day.'

They both turned to the door as Greg's mother walked in.

'What's going on here?' she said, her eyebrows raised. She wore a gold sheath dress; a small evening bag in the same fabric hung from her arm on a gold chain.

'You look lovely, Mum.'

'Thank you, Greg. It's not often I get complimented on my appearance.' She smiled at her husband.

'You know you always look nice, love.' He glanced across at Greg, his eyebrows raised.

'Yes, Dad. You can tell her.'

'Tell me what? You're not going to France anymore?'

'Yes, I am, but I'm going back to university next year. I'm going to study law.'

His mother's smile was as wide as his father's, and Greg knew he had made the right decision. In his heart, he knew that was the career path he wanted to take.

'Anyway, it's time I left. How long till you go?'

'We're going now; no time for your sherry, Madeleine,' Dad said. 'Drive safe, son; that road back from Duckinwilla can be pretty bad at night. Watch out for the roos.'

'I will, Dad. It's good to be home.' He shook his father's hand and kissed his mother, anticipation building as he headed out to the car.

Greg grinned as he slid behind the wheel. He was going home in more ways than one—to the career he'd been avoiding, to the family he'd been distant from, and maybe, just maybe, towards something unexpected with a woman in a yellow dress who made him want to sing along with the radio.

CHAPTER 10

Her grandparent's house

Charlotte sat on the edge of her bed in Grandmère's house, her heart still racing from the conversation with her grandparents earlier. The room was filled with the perpetual scent of lavender wafting in from the garden outside, but anxiety roiled in her stomach. Just as she was about to clear her mind and call Greg, her phone rang.

She smiled the whole time she was talking to him, and when she disconnected, she hurried down the hall to find Grandmère in the kitchen, her back turned as she arranged a bouquet of fresh flowers.

'Grandmère,' Charlotte called, stepping into the room. 'We do have an extra guest for dinner tonight.'

'Oh? And who may that be?' Grandmère's smile was curious.

'Greg,' Charlotte replied, her cheeks warming. 'He's going to come to support me. Is that alright?'

Grandmère raised an eyebrow, her expression a mix of amusement and intrigue. 'Do you think that will make Lisette behave, or is jealousy your motive?'

'Neither,' Charlotte said quickly. 'I genuinely enjoy Greg's company. I just thought—it might help ease the tension. Having someone not family beside me.'

'Very well, my dear,' Grandmère said, her voice laced with wisdom. 'It sounds like a delightful plan. It's good to have someone else there for you. Now, you look tired. I'll take you up to the guest room and run you a deep bubble bath. I want you to relax.'

'That sounds lovely, but would you mind if I go back to *Maison de Rêve*, ?'

'Of course not, *ma chérie*. Let me pack you a few things to take with you.'

'I'll be back here in an hour and a half, Grandmère.'

'Yes, but I want you to look your absolute best tonight.'

##

Charlotte was soon back at *Maison de Rêve*,

She opened one of the two bags Grandmère had handed her as she left: two fluffy towels, face washers, a hand towel, a bath mat, and some French bubble bath. She looked at the deep bath in the small bathroom and then at the bottle of bubble bath that Grandmère had packed, and she smiled. She put in the plug and turned the taps on full as she reached the bottom of the bag. There was a small bottle of champagne in there, along with a wineglass, and her smile grew; Grandmère was an absolute gem.

Since she had spent time with her grandparents, Charlotte was much calmer. She knew whatever happened, she would give it her best, and if her mother wanted to stay alienated, that was her choice. She had done nothing wrong, and tonight—in public, in front of the family—she would state that fact. After dinner, she intended to step outside and try to talk to Lisette. If her sister wouldn't listen, so be it.

Excitement bubbled away as she unfolded the towels and put them in the bathroom. She loved this house, and if things had been different, she would have considered moving in. She would insist on paying rent because she didn't want to give her siblings any idea that she was getting unfair benefits from their grandparents.

How sad was it to have to worry about that?

One thing that did worry her was how unwell Dad looked, and that was another reason to try to make peace. She'd have a talk with Mum, too, and see what was going on.

Charlotte's excitement grew as she took one last look in the mirror. All of the nervousness she'd held about having dinner with the family had dissipated, and she was very much looking forward to having Greg beside her tonight. The fact that he had accepted her invitation and agreed to accompany her to dinner—despite the potential awkwardness—made her heart swell with happiness.

She knew, after working with him for a year, that he was a good person. He had always been kind to the staff, even when making policy decisions that could be unpopular. All in all, he was a very nice man, and the attraction that had been growing all year was starting to blossom. Now that they weren't working together, she wouldn't fight that attraction.

The thought that Greg would be travelling to France at the same time as she was made her happy. She wondered how long he was going to stay there, especially since he had decided not to go back to school.

The crunch of tyres on the gravel driveway outside had her hurrying to the window. She smiled as she looked at the car in the driveway; Greg had good taste in cars. She hadn't known that he drove an Audi, too. She smoothed down the emerald green silk dress she was wearing and reached up to check that her hair was still smooth. She had put in the effort with her makeup, shadowing her eyes in dark green and wearing pale lipstick tonight. The emerald green complemented her auburn hair and fair skin, and she knew she looked good. She needed to look good for her confidence, and she felt that all would be well.

Charlotte hurried down the stairs and across the foyer, opening the door before Greg could knock. 'Come in,' she said, 'and please excuse the state of the house. It hasn't been lived in for a year or two.'

'It's a beautiful house,' he said, looking around. 'It might be old, but it has great bones.'

Charlotte smiled. 'That's what Papa used to say. He built it when they first moved here. I think it would've been in the 1970s.'

'It's beautiful. How come you're staying here?' he asked. 'Is the family situation that bad?'

'No, I just needed some space. I stayed here last night, too.'

He stood back and took her hands. 'You look absolutely stunning, Charlotte. I hope you don't mind me saying that.'

'That's lovely, thank you.'

'That's the second time I've complimented a woman on her appearance this evening. My mum and dad are going to Maryborough for dinner, and Mum looked pretty good, too.'

'I'm sure she appreciated you saying it.'

'She did. Things have been good at home this afternoon.' He nodded as he let her hands go. 'I told Dad what my plans were for next year, and I don't think I'll hear any complaints from the family for quite a while.'

'You've made your plans?'

'I have. I'll tell you about it later. Let's get moving so we can get this dinner over and done with.'

CHAPTER 11

Her grandparent's house

Greg turned the Audi into the cul-de-sac that Charlotte pointed out to him as they headed back towards Duckinwilla Creek. It was an upscale estate with lots of houses on sizeable lots that he hadn't realised were around here. She pointed up the hill. 'Grandmère and Papa's house is at the top, at the end of the cul-de-sac. Just turn into the drive. There's a circular driveway and a little parking area on the left-hand side. I'm sure there'll be a few cars there already, so just . . .' she pointed. 'That's right, this one parked next to the white ute—that's Julien's. I'm pleased he's here already. A little bit more moral support.'

'Are you nervous?' he asked.

'No, I'm feeling good. And thank you, Greg,' she reached out for his hand as he turned off the Audi. 'I really appreciate your support. It was a big ask and probably a bit out there.'

'No, Charlotte, I really enjoy your company, and I hope our friendship can grow.' His eyes held hers, and she knew there was something on his side as well. Warmth filtered through her body as he held her gaze.

'Are you ready to go in?'

'Yep, let's do this.'

'Wait there,' he said as she sat in the passenger seat; then he walked around and opened her door. He glanced over at the house, opened the door and held out his hand to her. Charlotte took it and climbed gracefully out of the car, clutching her small bag. The emerald silk felt good against her skin; the silk rustled softly as she walked beside Greg. He stopped and put his hand on her elbow. 'Do you think anyone will be watching from inside?'

'Quite possibly. It depends if Lisette is there or not. I'm not sure what she drives.'

'In that case, we'll put on a show.' He leaned forward and brushed his lips across hers. 'Thank you for inviting me tonight.'

As he pulled back, there was a sparkle in her eyes that made his heart race.

He took her hand, and they walked across the paved circular driveway and past the fountain in the centre. As they reached the front door, it opened, and Charlotte's grandparents ushered them in.

Their welcome was warm, and as Greg was introduced to the rest of the family, her grandmother worked hard to put everyone at ease. Greg was struck by the way Margot engaged with everyone. Her gentle laughter rang out like music, and it was clear how much the family respected their grandmother.

Even Charlotte's sister, Lisette. Her eyes narrowed when they were introduced, but she had been polite.

Conversation over drinks was lively, and Greg could see Charlotte relaxing, although her glance darted towards her parents a few times. They sat quietly and didn't speak much.

When she spoke about teaching French, her passion lit up her eyes. 'It's been hard work, but I've really enjoyed the last two years,' she said, her voice animated.

Greg chuckled softly in agreement. 'She's a very good teacher too! I've seen her in action, and she makes learning fun and engaging,' he said, eager to support her.

After half an hour, Margot summoned them to the large dining room table.

Greg settled into his seat beside Charlotte at the long table in her grandmother's elegantly decorated dining room. The soft golden light from the chandeliers cast a warm glow, creating a cosy atmosphere that felt welcoming. Nerves had kicked in when they walked into a full living room, but he had soon been put at his ease, and having Charlotte by his side eased his tension. She looked beautiful, her smile brightening the room as she introduced him to her grandparents, her parents, and the rest of her family.

As Charlotte sat beside him, the warm ambience of the room contrasted with the tension that was still there. The food was superb. The woman who had cooked the meal had outdone herself: hors d'oeuvres, soup, then Beef Wellington with baked vegetables, and now she had just brought out a huge Bombe Alaska.

Greg smiled when Charlotte sat back, placing her hands on her stomach. 'Oh, my goodness, I don't think I can eat any more.'

'You need fattening up, girl,' her father said. 'You're way too thin. You've been working too hard.'

He looked at Greg with a measured expression, and Greg knew Charlotte would be answering some questions later on.

***

Charlotte sat beside Greg at the table. The conversations around the table were loud, but Lisette remained subdued. Charlotte noticed her sister's eyes flicking to Greg and then back to her, and every time Charlotte caught her eye, Lisette looked down, a hint of anxiety crossing her face.

Emily was delightful, sitting on Charlotte's left, with Julien on her other side. Julien had made a good choice. She and Emily chatted away so enthusiastically that eventually, Grandmère interrupted, saying, 'May we have a conversation with you two girls as well?' She smiled, her eyes twinkling with warmth.

'Oh, I'm sorry, Margot,' Emily replied. 'It's just that Charlotte and I are getting to know each other.'

'I hope she's not telling you my childhood secrets,' Julien chimed in playfully.

'You'd be surprised,' Charlotte quipped back at him.

Charlotte noticed the interest that Dad was showing in Greg. He had been a fabulous companion, and she was pleased she'd asked him to come. She would tell Dad that Greg was a friend if he asked.

If he cared.

There was no point in delving into any relationship details—not that there was anything to tell—especially since she was heading off to France soon.

The dessert was eaten, and a cheese platter was brought out, accompanied by two pots of coffee. Grandmère cleared her throat, drawing everyone's attention. The soft conversation ceased, and everyone waited with anticipation.

'Family,' Grandmère began, her dignified presence filling the space, 'I have an announcement to make. This Saturday night, we are having a community function at the hall to farewell Charlotte before she heads to France.'

Charlotte's eyes widened, and she put a hand to her chest. A farewell gathering? She had expected a few quiet goodbyes, but the thought of the whole community gathering for her overwhelmed her.

'That's so lovely, Grandmère,' she exclaimed. 'I appreciate everyone's support, but please, no function.'

'Nonsense, *ma chèrie*,' Grandmère replied, her gaze steady. 'You have always been a part of this community, and they want to celebrate your new journey. It's an opportunity for everyone to show their love and support, just as you've always done for them.'

Before Charlotte could respond, she caught movement from the corner of her eye. Lisette had straightened in her chair, her expression shifting as the implications of Grandmère's words sank in.

'What do you mean, farewell? It's not like she's going to some distant place,' Lisette said sharply, her voice dripping with disdain. 'You're acting as if she's some sort of hero, and now everyone needs to come and say goodbye. It's absolutely ridiculous!'

Charlotte's cheeks burned at Lisette's harsh tone, the familiar knot of tension tightening in her stomach. 'Lisette, it's just—'

'Just? Just what? You think this is all about you, don't you?' Lisette snapped, eyes flashing with irritation. 'You're leaving us again, just like before. Why should the whole town make a fuss over it? It's embarrassing. It's always about you.'

'They're not making a fuss over just me,' Charlotte said quietly.

Lisette scoffed. 'Not making a fuss? They're

throwing a party? You don't think the entire town knows what you did? They're just curious to see how this whole charade plays out!'

'Lisette, please,' Julien interjected gently, trying to diffuse the situation. 'This is a family dinner for Charlotte, not a platform to air grievances. And we have a guest.'

Charlotte straightened as tension crackled in the air.

'Grandmère, may we be excused for a moment?' Charlotte asked.

'Of course, my dear,' her grandmother replied, her eyes full of concern.

Charlotte glanced across the table at her sister, who was sitting up from Julien on the other side, between Oliver and Guy. 'Right, Lisette, would you come outside with me, please?' Determination flowed through her, and her tone meant business. 'A chat that's long overdue.'

Lisette's eyes widened, and she looked scared.

Grandmère looked at Lisette and said, 'Go, my child.'

Charlotte stood up. Greg reached for her hand and squeezed it, his reassuring touch giving her the strength she needed.

There was a small balcony adjacent to the dining room, and Charlotte opened the sliding doors and walked out. Lisette followed her, her arms folded and her glare holding malice. The balcony doors closed behind them with a soft click, leaving Charlotte and Lisette alone under the star-filled Queensland sky. Below, the lights of Duckinwilla Creek twinkled like fallen stars, the town seemingly peaceful from this distance.

'What's with you and the guy from Dunmora?' Lisette came on the attack right away.

'Greg and I are friends,' Charlotte said firmly. 'We worked together in Brisbane.'

'What do you want to talk about?'

'I think we need to clear the air. I don't want to go to France feeling like I have for the past few years. We need to address this situation between us. I want to do it tonight so the family can see we're *both* making an effort. I'm sure you haven't been happy either. So tell me, why do you hate me so much?'

'I don't hate you. I just hate what you did.'

'What did I do? It was you who stole my boyfriend.'

'It wasn't that. Brett did the wrong thing by coming on to me while he was still with you,' Lisette said begrudgingly. 'I know that.'

'He did. And you were only fifteen. You were underage. He could have been charged.'

'Nothing happened.' Lisette looked away, but Charlotte knew that sly look her sister got when she was lying. She'd seen it many times when they were growing up.

'Really?'

'Well, maybe, but don't you dare tell Mum and Dad. You want to know why I really hate you?' Lisette's voice trembled. 'Because you left. You just ran away and left me to deal with everything.'

'Left you to deal with what, Lisette? With the lies that you and Brett obviously told about me? Lies that I don't even know, so I can't defend myself.'

'You don't understand. You never understood.' Lisette wrapped her arms around herself. 'Brett was working at the store that summer, remember? He told me things—about the missing money, about how you were helping him cook the books because you thought the family wasn't sophisticated enough for you.'

'What!' Charlotte's chest tightened. 'And you believed him? Your own sister?'

'I was only fifteen! And you were always so . . . perfect. Grandmère's favourite, Dad's pride and joy, the one who was going to university, the one who was going to escape this town.' Bitterness edged Lisette's words. 'Brett said you were planning to take the money and run away to France anyway. He made it sound like I was protecting the family by backing up his story.'

'The missing money that nearly destroyed the store? That gave Dad his first heart turn? Julien told me about that, but I never had any idea that I had been blamed. *You* told them I was responsible for that? You let them believe that?' Charlotte put a hand to her chest, trying to take air into her lungs.

'Brett showed me the altered books with your signature. He said if I didn't back him up, Dad would lose everything.' Tears spilled down Lisette's cheeks. 'I was so scared, Charlotte. And then when everything exploded, and Dad collapsed . . . it was easier to keep lying than admit what we'd done.'

'It's all lies. I knew nothing about any money. I signed nothing! What about Mum?

How could she believe the worst of me? She's my mother; she knew me inside and out, and yet you managed to make her believe that?'

Lisette's laugh was hollow. 'Because you're everything she fears, Charlie. You're Grandmère's granddaughter through and through—sophisticated, ambitious, French. Mum's always felt like an outsider in this family, and you . . . you remind her of everything she's not.'

The truth of it hit Charlotte like a physical blow. All these years, she'd thought it was just about Brett, about teenage jealousy. But the roots went so much deeper. She'd left town because she thought everyone had blamed *her* for dumping Brett. No wonder she could never understand the depth of the rift. All this time, her parents thought she was a thief. She would bet that they hadn't told Grandmère.

'Brett took over ten thousand dollars,' Charlotte said quietly. 'Dad nearly lost the store. His heart has never been the same.'

'And you've let them blame me for five years.'

'I was trapped! The longer it went on, the harder it was to tell the truth. And Brett threatened to tell everyone about what happened between us if I ever spoke up. He said I encouraged him, and he would be the one to go to jail because I was only fifteen. And I didn't want Dad to know that he—you know what.'

'That he had sex with an underage girl?' Charlotte's stomach lurched. 'You were fifteen, Lisette. Whatever happened, he took advantage of you.'

'I know that now.' Lisette's voice broke. 'I see him sometimes in Maryborough. He's got a new scam going with some other business. And every time I see him, I remember what I helped him do to you, to our family.'

'Does anyone else know the truth?'

'Julien suspected. That's why he was happy to take over the store—to figure out exactly what happened. He's the one who eventually caught Brett's pattern, but you were long gone, and the damage was done.'

'And he didn't tell Dad?'

'He was worried about Dad having another heart attack because you'd been blamed. It was all water under the bridge by then, and Dad recovered. We didn't want to risk his health.'

'So I was the fall guy,' Charlotte said

bitterly.

'You had everything, Charlotte. Grandmère and Papa paid for you to go to university, you were living in the city, and you had a great job. And now you're going to France.'

'Everything? I paid my own way. I had no family,' Charlotte said quietly, knowing she was going to have to find the strength to forgive Lisette, but she could understand why her sister had believed Brett's lies at first. 'And Brett was never charged.' Understanding dawned. 'I wondered why Julien gave up his dream of being a chef. To protect Dad from it happening again.'

'Julien's been trying to fix everything I broke.' Tears spilled down Lisette's cheeks. 'And now Rowena—she's threatening to tell everyone about Brett and me unless Julien—'

'Unless Julien what?'

'It doesn't matter. That's not relevant to this. It's not a part of it.' Lisette looked away.

Charlotte stepped forward, taking her sister's hands. 'Then help me fix it. Tell Mum and Dad the truth—all of it. Let me help you make this right.'

'Mum will never forgive me.'

'Maybe not right away. But this secret is

poisoning our family, Lisette. Look what it did to Dad's health, and to Julien, and to you.'

And to me.

For a long moment, only the chirp of crickets broke the silence. Then Lisette squared her shoulders. 'Okay,' she whispered. 'Okay. But will you help me tell them?'

Charlotte squeezed her hands. 'That's what big sisters are for. But not now. We'll tell everyone we've made up, and we'll see Mum and Dad privately tomorrow.

'Okay.' Lisette stopped and put her hand on Charlotte's arm. 'It's so good to have you home.

The truth was finally going to come out. She was still in shock. As they turned back toward the dining room, Charlotte caught Greg's eye through the window. His steady gaze gave her strength. Whatever came next, she wasn't alone anymore.

'We should go back in. Mum will be stressing,' Lisette said with a shaky smile.

'And Grandmère.'

Together, they walked back into the dining room, where a curious silence met them. She sat straight and spoke firmly. 'Right everyone, Lisette and I have had a chat, and we've sorted our differences.'

Grandmère smiled. '*Bien fait, les filles.*'

Papa stood. 'Well done, girls!'

Charlotte looked at her parents; her mother looked away, but Dad smiled at her. He was looking better tonight, although his skin had a blotchy pallor, and she noticed that he hadn't eaten much. She'd follow that up tomorrow when she and Lisette went over to talk to them.

Greg reached for her hand and squeezed it, this time not letting go; Charlotte's happiness almost bubbled over, warming her from the inside out.

She glanced at Julien; he was staring out of the window, looking as though his thoughts were miles away. Maybe he needed to have a chat with Lisette as well.

CHAPTER 12

Maison de Rêve

Greg pulled up outside the front door at *Maison de Rêve*.

'Thank you, Greg. You'll never know how grateful I am to you for taking me tonight.'

'It turned into a good night after all of your worry,' he replied, a warm smile spreading across his face.

'It did, and I finally got things sorted with Lisette. I just need to see Mum and Dad tomorrow and talk to them. I'm worried about them, and I need to get things sorted there before I can focus on France.' She would tell Greg what had ensued after Mum and Dad had found out the truth.

'Don't forget you've got your big farewell function on Saturday night. Your grandmother invited me too. Is that okay with you?'

'Of course it is! And you know what? I'm excited about it now. I think there might be some surprises in store for me. Julien hinted at some special guests that I'm going to be pleased to see, but he wouldn't tell me who they were.'

'It sounds like it's going to be a good night.'

As Greg opened the car door for her, a massive clap of thunder boomed overhead, followed by a bright flash of lightning.

'Oh wow, look at those clouds boiling over the mountain,' she said. 'Quick, come inside with me. I'll make a coffee before you head back.'

Greg followed her into the kitchen at the back of the house as she began searching the cupboards for a coffee maker. The kitchen was bare, but the essentials were still there. Charlotte opened the small bag that Grandma had given her as they left after dinner and smiled. Inside were some coffee granules, long-life milk, sugar, and a small box of chocolates. 'I'm certainly well looked after,' she said.

They stood together at the kitchen window as the coffee brewed, watching the sheets of torrential rain sweep across the back garden, the sound almost drowning out conversation.

'This is flood rain,' he said, his brow furrowing with concern. 'In fact, perhaps I should go now because there are a couple of creeks I have to cross on the other side of the mountain to get home.'

Charlotte frowned. 'It doesn't sound safe. It's very late.' She bit her lip and hesitated, torn between the anxiety of his safety and the desire to keep him close. 'Perhaps you could stay the night,' she suggested, holding up her hands in a gesture of innocence. 'I mean, just stay the night in the spare room. I'm not making a move on you,' she added with a mischievous grin.

The coffee machine clicked off, but before she could move towards it, Greg's arms wrapped around her waist, pulling her against him.

Greg gave her a knowing smile. 'I wouldn't mind if you were making a move,' he whispered, his voice low and filled with intent. The words hung between them, and before Charlotte could respond, he moved closer.

His hand gently cupped her face, tilting her chin up. The space between them vanished, and their lips met in a kiss—soft at first, tender, and then, it deepened, yet still filled with sweetness. The kiss was a promise, a quiet agreement shared between them without a single word spoken.

When they finally parted, their foreheads rested against one another. Neither spoke for a moment, but the need to be close—to be together—went without saying.

Charlotte's pulse raced, and with a smile that bordered on teasing, she whispered, 'There's only one bed made up.'

Greg chuckled softly, his fingers brushing through her hair. 'What a shame,' he said, his voice a whisper against her lips. 'And the water for the coffee's gone cold, too. What will we do?'

He kissed her again, this time with more urgency, his arms holding her against him. Charlotte was caught between happiness and desire; she knew exactly what they would do. As she led Greg upstairs, his hand holding hers tightly, there was no sound apart from their breathing.

All the while, she smiled to herself. The coffee, after all, could wait.

##

The next morning, Charlotte awoke to soft dawn light filtering through the curtains, the sounds of the storm replaced by the gentle chirping of birds outside. She turned to find Greg beside her, a peaceful expression on his face as he slept. Her eyes roved over his features—his dark lashes resting against his tanned skin, the faint stubble on his jaw adding a rugged edge to his otherwise serene face. She couldn't help but trace the line of his lips as an ache of longing stirred deep within her. In that warm moment, contentment and a glimpse of the future filled her. She knew it wasn't too soon—everything about them felt right. She put her head next to his and closed her eyes as happiness filled her. She could face anything today; even the talk with Mum and Dad.

The morning light filled the room, casting a warm glow over everything when she woke the second time. She stirred awake, the soft goose-down mattress cradling her like a cloud. As her eyes fluttered open, she looked up to find Greg lying beside her, propped up on one elbow, a playful grin spreading across his face.

'Good morning, sleepyhead,' he said, his voice low and smooth as honey.

'Good morning,' she murmured, still slightly dazed.

He tilted his head, looking at her with a combination of affection and mischief. 'You know, I've been meaning to tell you something.'

Charlotte blinked, her heart racing at the prospect of his confession. 'What's that?'

Greg shifted closer, resting his head on his hand while gazing earnestly into her eyes. 'I've been fighting this attraction to you for the past year. It was like trying to hold back a tidal wave, and it took a lot of doing. Maybe I should have given in back then.'

Her breath caught in her throat. 'You too?' she confessed, a soft smile breaking on her lips. 'I never wanted to acknowledge it either. I thought it was just me being foolish or impulsive. I mean, falling for the boss?'

'Foolish? Hardly. I mean, look at us,' he chuckled softly. 'It took us this long to get here. The universe has a funny way of pushing us together, don't you think?'

Charlotte nodded, her heart swelling with both excitement and trepidation. 'It's kind of coincidental. You coming to France?'

Greg's expression grew serious, a hint of sincerity lining his features. 'To be honest, I only planned the trip to France because I knew you'd be over there. I was hoping to see you—maybe run into you at a café or something. I knew what school you were going to because I wrote the reference.'

Charlotte's breath caught again, a rush of

warmth flooding her cheeks. 'Really? You would have come looking for me?'

'Absolutely,' he replied earnestly. 'I want to spend more time with you, Charlotte, wherever that might lead.'

'Well, a picnic sounds good,' she said with a teasing smile. 'What's the plan for today?'

Greg chuckled, the sound rich and warm. 'I have to head back to my parents' house this morning. But I'd love to take you out for a picnic later—if that's okay with you.'

Charlotte nodded. 'That sounds perfect! I'll be ready for a break from the whirlwind of family drama. Things should be a bit easier since Lisette and I sorted everything out last night.' She shifted, propping herself up on her elbow to face him better. 'So, what are your plans after France?'

Greg's expression changed, his voice becoming more thoughtful. 'Well, I'm planning to go back to university and study law.'

Charlotte felt a pang of bittersweet sadness. 'That's amazing! But—it makes me sad to think about how I'll be in France for six months, and you'll be back here in Australia.'

Greg reached out, gently tucking a loose

strand of hair behind her ear. 'Life has its twists and turns, but I believe we can make this work. You never know what could happen in six months.'

Later, they sat on the balcony, enjoying a coffee together as they looked out over the lush valley of Duckinwilla Creek. The view of the rolling hills and trees was breathtaking, and Charlotte's contentment grew as she sipped her coffee.

'This is perfect. I feel like I've woken up from five years of sleep,' she said softly, savouring the moment. The crisp air filled her lungs as she took in the beauty around her. 'Woken up by the kiss of a prince.'

'As long as it wasn't a frog,' Greg replied, a happy grin on his face as he watched her. 'I feel so lucky to be here with you already. It's fast-forwarded all my expectations.'

'Meant to be.' Charlotte looked at him, returning his happy smile as he put his hand on hers.

CHAPTER 13

Sunlight streamed through the windows as Charlotte hummed softly.

Her phone buzzed: Lisette. **At the farm. Mum's in the kitchen. You coming?**

Charlotte took a deep breath. **On my way.**

Greg appeared in the doorway, hair damp from the shower. 'Ready?'

'As I'll ever be.' She reached for him, drawing strength from his solid presence. 'Thank you for staying.'

'Wild horses couldn't have dragged me away.' He kissed her softly. 'Want me to come with you?'

'No, this needs to be just family. But—' She smiled up at him. 'Picnic lunch?'

'Try and stop me.'

The drive to the farm was too short. Charlotte's hands tightened on the steering wheel as she pulled up beside Lisette's car. Her sister waited on the back steps, pale but determined.

'You look different,' Lisette said quietly.

Heat crept up Charlotte's neck. 'Good different?'

'Happy different.' A ghost of a smile touched Lisette's lips. 'Greg's good for you.'

They found their mother in the kitchen, aggressively kneading bread dough. Ellen's shoulders stiffened as they entered, but she didn't turn around.

'Mum?' Lisette's voice shook. 'We need to talk to you.'

'Your father's resting,' Ellen said sharply. 'He didn't sleep well. He's worried about you being here, Charlotte.'

'This can't wait, Mum.' Charlotte said gently. 'It's about the money. About what really happened five years ago.'

Ellen's hands stilled in the dough. 'I don't want to hear it.'

'You need to.' Lisette stepped forward. 'Because it wasn't Charlotte. It was Brett. He stole the money, and I—I helped him cover it up.'

The colour drained from Ellen's face. She gripped the counter, leaving floury handprints. 'What are you saying?'

'He manipulated me, Mum. I was fifteen and stupid and jealous, and he showed me how to alter the books to make it look like Charlotte's fault. And then when Dad had his heart turn—' Lisette's voice broke.

'All this time?' Ellen's whisper was harsh. 'You let us blame Charlotte all this time?'

'I was scared,' Lisette sobbed. 'Brett threatened to tell everyone about—about what happened between us. And then Dad got sick, and I couldn't—'

'Couldn't what?' Hugo stood there, one hand pressed to his chest, his face grey.

'Dad!' Charlotte rushed to him. 'You should be resting.'

'I heard.' His voice was thin, strained. 'I heard everything.'

'Hugo, please,' Ellen started forward, but he waved her off.

'My own daughters.' He swayed slightly, and Charlotte slipped an arm around him. 'One betrayed by a man I trusted in my store. The other too young to know better. And I blamed the wrong one.'

'Daddy, please sit down.' Lisette grabbed a kitchen chair. 'Your colour's not good.'

He sank into it, still clutching his chest. Ellen hovered, her face a mask of worry and confusion. 'Should I call the doctor?'

'No.' Hugo reached for Charlotte's hand. 'I need to say this. I'm sorry, love. I should have trusted you. Should have looked harder for the truth.'

'It doesn't matter now,' Charlotte said quietly, but he shook his head.

'It matters. Letting you go, believing the worst . . . that's on me. Your mother and I, we—'

'We were wrong,' Ellen finished quietly. She opened a bottle and passed a tablet to Hugo. He put it under his tongue and closed his eyes. She still wouldn't quite meet Charlotte's gaze, but something had shifted in her stance. 'About so many things.'

Hugo's grip on Charlotte's hand tightened, but as the medication took effect, his colour slowly improved. After a few minutes, he opened his eyes, looking steadier.

'Dad?' Charlotte studied his face with concern. 'You're not well, are you?'

'I've got an appointment with a specialist in Brisbane next week,' he admitted. 'Your mother's been fussing over me something fierce.'

'With good reason,' Ellen said, her voice

softening as she touched his shoulder. 'You need to take better care of yourself.'

Hugo looked between his daughters, then opened his arms. 'Come here, both of you.'

Charlotte and Lisette moved into their father's embrace, and for a moment, they were children again, safe in his strong arms. Through her tears, Charlotte caught her mother's eye and saw something there—not quite forgiveness yet, but perhaps the beginning of understanding.

'My girls,' Hugo murmured, holding them close. 'No more secrets, hey? This family's had enough of those.'

Charlotte nodded against his shoulder, breathing in the familiar scent of him, thankful that the truth hadn't cost them more than it had. There would be time to heal, to rebuild.

Time to be a family again.

CHAPTER 14

The soft burble of the creek mingled with the laughter of birds flitting among the trees, creating a serene backdrop for the afternoon picnic. Sunlight filtered through the leaves, dappling the ground with playful patterns and warming Charlotte and Greg as they lounged on a checkered picnic rug. Surrounded by lush greenery and the sweet scent of wildflowers, the creek sparkled nearby, inviting them to dip their toes in its gentle flow.

Charlotte lay back, a soft sigh escaping her lips as she traced circles in the river sand with her finger. With a smile, she turned to Greg, who was propped up on one elbow, casually tossing bits of grass into the water.

'Are you looking forward to Saturday night?' he asked, his voice punctuating the tranquil atmosphere.

'I am,' Charlotte admitted, but there was a hint of hesitation in her tone. 'Still, I can't shake the feeling that the gossip mill is going to be in full swing. People just don't understand what it was like for me. They want to label everything as right or wrong when life isn't that simple.'

Greg raised an eyebrow, considering her words. 'Sure, it might have felt monumental for you, but to the community, it was just a broken relationship. They didn't know what Lisette did. You were young and headed off to university. I doubt it was the scandal you're imagining.'

Charlotte nodded slowly, her brow furrowing in thought. 'I get that now, but back then, it consumed me. Leaving was a whirlwind; I had no idea how messed up everything would get. If I had, I'd still be here.'

'And we wouldn't have met.'

'We wouldn't.' Charlotte bit her lip, her uncertainty re-emerging. 'Part of me feels like I've moved on, yet another part feels so unresolved. Did I make a mistake in leaving so suddenly? Did I give up too easily?'

'Your past does not define you, Charlotte,' Greg reassured her, gently brushing a stray hair from her face. 'Whatever happens, just make sure it's right for you. Enjoy your farewell.'

His words brought a faint smile to her lips as gratitude filled her. 'You're right.'

Greg laughed softly, coaxing her spirits higher. 'Maybe this is their way of trying to say sorry. You know how gossip works in small towns—there's a new story every day. I'm sure everyone who's coming will be there to wish you the best.'

Feeling lighter than she had in days, Charlotte joined in his laughter. 'You are a wise man. This picnic is lovely, and spending this time with you has helped more than I can say.'

'Julien can certainly cook.' Her brother had put a picnic basket together for them.

Seeing Charlotte relax was a joy for Greg, and he smiled as the soft sounds of nature surrounded them.

'I can't believe how quickly everything is sorting itself out,' she continued, her excitement blooming. 'And with us flying to France together—what a twist!'

Greg's grin broadened. 'It's like the universe has been nudging us towards this moment. The thought of exploring those quaint streets with you feels like a dream.'

Charlotte laughed lightly, her eyes sparkling with joy. 'I never expected all of this to happen. Grandmère and Papa were shocked when Lisette went to see them and told them the truth. She went there before she went to Mum and Dad's this morning.'

'You are very special to your grandparents. They trusted you.'

'They are special to me too. Even Mum seems to be coming around, although slowly. Maybe she's finally realising that I'm not the same girl who left home.'

'She must be worried about your dad.'

'Yes, I'll be pleased when he goes to see the specialist. I can't get anything out of either of them. I think Grandmère knows something, but she won't say either. She sounded worried when she called me. I asked her, but she closed down.'

'Maybe your mum just needs time to adjust. She'll see how happy you are, and it will all fall into place.'

'I do love your optimism, Greg.' Charlotte beamed at him, her heart lighter. 'It feels wonderful. You've lifted a weight from my shoulders. I can almost see a brighter future ahead for us.'

'I haven't done anything.' He held her eyes with his. 'Apart from falling in love with you.'

His words hung between them like a promise, and the world around them faded into a gentle blur as Greg leaned in, and Charlotte met him halfway, their lips brushing softly in a tender kiss. It was gentle and unhurried, a sweet declaration of a future.

CHAPTER 15

Duckinwilla Creek Community Hall

Over the next few days, Greg and Charlotte spent most of their time together. Every second night, he stayed at *Maison de Rêve* with her, and their relationship deepened in ways neither of them had anticipated. Warmth filled her whenever she was near him, a sense of belonging she'd been missing since she left home.

Greg had changed his flights so that they would be flying to France together. They planned to have a holiday before Charlotte had to start work at the school, and the thought filled her with excitement. The prospect of exploring new places with him felt like a dream come true.

The week flew by, and soon it was Saturday night. Days spent with Greg had been wonderful, and he looked happier now that he and his father had sorted out their differences. Greg shared with her that he had submitted all of his university applications and was excited to tell Charlotte that when he returned from his holiday, he would be starting a few hours a week at his father's office in Maryborough.

'I can do a lot of the degree remotely. I'll just have to go down to Brisbane a few times a year,' he explained.

Charlotte reached up and cupped his cheek, her heart swelling with pride. 'You look so much happier and relaxed. I think you've made the right decision.'

'I'll miss you, Charlotte,' he said, his expression turning sombre.

'I'll miss you too,' she replied, her voice soft. 'You know, in some ways, I wish I wasn't going. Now that I'm home, I feel as though I should stay longer. But I've got the contract; I have to go.'

'You'll enjoy every minute of it, and we'll have some time together there first before I come home.'

A mixture of excitement and regret filled Charlotte as the day of the farewell approached. She couldn't believe how many were coming; Julien and the girls had catered for finger food and drinks for over a hundred friends and community—it seemed everyone she hadn't seen in years was coming. Even two of her old school teachers from Maryborough had been invited, and she wondered whether the family had gone a bit over the top. But when Grandmère organised something, it had to be the best.

'Are you nearly ready, Charlotte? I thought you wanted to be there before everyone arrived,' Greg called out from downstairs. They were getting ready at *Maison de Rêve.* When Charlotte had decided to stay there, Grandmère had organised a maintenance man and a cleaner to come and tidy up, despite Charlotte's protests that she'd only be there for two weeks.

'I do. I just can't decide what to wear,' she shouted back, standing in her underwear as she stared at the four dresses that had remained untouched since she'd arrived. 'Come and help me choose, Greg.'

His footsteps thudded up the stairs, and she smiled as he appeared in the doorway. 'I really don't know what to wear. You pick.'

He surveyed the four dresses hanging by the window. 'Okay, eeny, meeny, miney, mo,' he said playfully.

'No, don't pick like that! You tell me which one looks the best, okay?'

'I like the yellow one,' he said, his eyes lighting up. 'It's nice and fresh, and it makes you look sunny and happy. And it goes with the colour of your hair. How's that?' He looked proud of himself.

'The yellow one it is!' she exclaimed, quickly reaching over to pull it over her underwear.

'That's a shame,' he teased.

'What's that? It's not good,' she said with a frown.

'No, you covered up that pretty underwear! I was enjoying looking at it.'

She reached over and tapped his shoulder. 'Enough of that—we have to go to town.'

***

Greg stood with Charlotte's younger brothers, Oliver and Guy, watching her as she walked around the room. She'd smiled more tonight than he had ever seen her smile; the shadows had gone from beneath her eyes. She looked genuinely happy and content. He nodded approvingly when he saw her hug Lisette. Amelia, her younger sister, trailed behind like a loyal shadow. Oliver nudged Greg lightly and whispered, 'There's a bit of hero worship there; Amelia adores Charlotte.'

'Not hard to do,' Greg said with a soft

chuckle. 'She's adorable.'

'So, what's the go with you two?' Oliver asked, curiosity in his tone.

'If I'm not overstepping the line, I think very highly of your sister,' Greg replied earnestly. 'I intend to spend a lot more time with her.'

'Even with her going away?'

'She'll be back,' Greg assured them.

Julien and Emily walked over to join them.

'You two are doing a fabulous job at the store,' Greg said. 'We've enjoyed your coffee and croissants a few times this week. I took some home to my parents, and I think they're making a special trip over next week to check out the General Store. The picnic you packed for Charlotte and me to take out to the national park the other day was superb.'

From across the room, Charlotte caught Greg's eye, and he smiled back as Charlotte pointed to her empty glass. He nodded.

'Drink, guys?' Greg asked. 'I'm heading over to the bar to grab another tonic water for Charlotte.'

'I'll have a white wine, thank you, Greg.' Emily linked her arm through Julien's.

'A beer for me,' Julien added.

'I'll come with you, and I'll take Charlotte's drink over if you like,' Emily said. 'I need to catch up with her; I haven't talked to her much tonight.'

'She's having a great time,' Greg said. 'She hasn't stopped smiling.'

'I think that has a lot to do with you,' Emily said with a grin. 'Although it has been a relief for her to get all that family stuff sorted. I don't think she'll stay away as long next time.'

It took a while for Greg to be served because of the crowd waiting for drinks. As he waited, he was struck by how many people lived in Duckinwilla Creek. It had turned into a fabulous night, filled with laughter and joyful reunions. Charlotte's Grandmère sat in her chair, holding court, and he was sure she had spoken to everyone who had come through the hall that night.

The big surprise for Charlotte had been the arrival of one of her best friends who'd travelled from the Northern Territory. When she'd walked in, Charlotte's scream filled the room, startling everyone. Greg turned, thinking something had gone wrong, but instead, he saw Charlotte hugging a tall woman with long black hair.

'Jenny!' she exclaimed. 'Oh my God, Jenny!'

When he was served, Greg handed the tonic water to Emily. 'I'll go back to Julien with the rest of the drinks while you go and find Charlotte.'

He juggled the tray, and as he crossed the hall, he noticed a woman he hadn't seen before standing with Julien. He hesitated to join them; their conversation seemed intense and serious.

But then Julien's face lost colour as he watched, and Greg's concern deepened. He glanced at their exchange, unsure of what was going on. Just then, the woman's voice rose above the crowd, and people near them turned to look. Lisette hurried over to them and spoke to the woman, but she shook her hand off her arm.

'You think you can just walk away from this, Julien?' the woman accused, her tone fierce.

'What are you talking about?' Julien stared at her. 'If it's about the store, this isn't the time to talk about it.'

'I'll have this conversation whenever I like. You have to stop avoiding me,' the woman shot back.

Greg stepped in, taking the woman's arm

gently but firmly. 'Perhaps it's not the time to have this conversation,' he said, trying to defuse the rising tension.

As he looked up, he spotted Emily walking back to them, her forehead set in a frown.

'It's your child, Julien Johnson and you're going to do something about it!' the woman shouted, her accusation hanging in the air like a thunderclap. Greg watched, his heart sinking, as Emily's hand shot to her mouth. Turning swiftly, she hurried out of the room, leaving a shocked silence in her wake.

CHAPTER 16

Duckinwilla Creek Community Hall

Charlotte glanced at her father, who stood beside the table with colourful decorations and loaded with plates of food, as she hurried across to Julien. She'd noticed Dad's pallor, too; he must have heard the confrontation between Julien and Rowena. The tension in the room still crackled from the words that everyone had overheard.

Rowena's words rang in her ears, and she could see Julien's distress.

The warm atmosphere was filled with laughter and chat from those who hadn't heard the conversation. Mum was bustling about, arranging snacks on the buffet table in the midst of several loud conversations around the table. Rowena's loud words hadn't reached that far. When she checked that Julien was okay, she'd see if Dad wanted to go outside for some quiet and fresh air.

Before she could walk over to Julien, their father clutched his chest suddenly, his hand shaking violently, causing a splash of punch to spill onto the tablecloth. A pained expression crossed his face, and he gasped for air, his eyes wide with fear as he staggered back and knocked a chair over.

'Dad!' Charlotte screamed, her voice cutting through the conversations. Everything slowed as she dashed toward him, desperate and frantic. Mum froze mid-motion, the colour draining from her face as she reached for the edge of the table for support.

Oliver and Guy leapt up from their seats, eyes wide with disbelief and horror as their father toppled backward, his body contorted in a way that sent shivers down Charlotte's spine. The cheerful atmosphere of the hall stilled, replaced by a harsh silence punctuated only by the sudden, shallow gasps of her father, each breath a frantic attempt to draw air.

The world spun around Charlotte, her heart pounding furiously as she watched Greg run across to Dad. He shoved chairs aside, creating space around her father, who was now lying motionless on the floor.

'Call triple zero!' Greg barked, dropping to his knees beside him, his face set with determination. His urgency snapped everyone into action, with Guy fumbling for his phone, fingers trembling as he dialled for help.

Greg began CPR, his hands pressing down rhythmically on Dad's chest. Charlotte looked around and saw the shock on Grandmère's face as her son lay fighting for his life. Papa had his arms around her, and she buried her face in his shoulder, shaking with sobs.

Charlotte's siblings stood beside their grandparents, Lisette and Amelia's tear-streaked faces reflecting her own panic. Mum grabbed her arm and clung tightly to her, murmuring reassurances that seemed to be more for herself than for anyone else. 'He'll be fine, Charlotte. The doctor said we didn't need to worry. It'll stop in a minute. Please, Hugo, listen to what he said.'

Charlotte gripped her mother's hand and watched as Greg worked, now aided by Julien, who had run over as soon as it was obvious that Dad was having a heart attack.

A heart attack. Nausea gripped Charlotte, but she knew she had to stay strong.

Oliver stood close to them, with one arm around Amelia, his shoulders tense and fists clenched, looking as though he felt utterly powerless. Lisette was beside them, both hands covering her mouth.

As the crowd began to gather, drawn by the commotion, silence descended on the hall. Charlotte stood there, willing time to move faster, praying for flashing lights and sirens—anything that would signal help was on the way for her father. At that moment, her world had narrowed to the desperate struggle for life unfolding before her.

CHAPTER 17

Maryborough Hospital – three days later

The sterile smell of antiseptic filled the air as Charlotte sat in the dimly lit hospital waiting room. The constant beeping of machines from the ICU echoed in her mind, a haunting reminder of her father's fragile state. It had been days since he was admitted, yet they still had no clear direction, only glimmers of hope that occasionally flickered like candlelight. His condition fluctuated, and the doctors could make no promises.

Her mind was a jumble of worries and regrets, looping endlessly as she struggled to make sense of everything. Just then, Julien appeared in the doorway, his expression haggard. He wasn't a tall man, but now he looked smaller and more vulnerable than Charlotte had ever seen him.

'Charlotte, I need to talk to you,' he said softly, gesturing for her to join him in the hall. She followed him, their footsteps echoing in the sterile corridor.

Once they were away from the others, Julien's composure seemed to crumble. 'I know I should stay,' he began, his voice raw with conflict. 'But I have to follow Emily to Sydney. I can't let her go. You, of all people, know how important it is not to let situations get out of control.'

Charlotte blinked in surprise. 'Have you spoken to her since she left?'

He nodded, the movement heavy with exhaustion. 'Yeah, she sent me a text saying she doesn't ever want to speak to me again. But she did say she hoped Dad was getting better.'

The news hit Charlotte hard. 'What's going on, Julien? Tell me about Rowena.'

Julien ran a shaking hand through his hair, the strands falling back into disarray. 'She's lying. All I know is that Emily doesn't believe me, and I can't believe that she doesn't trust me. I thought we were fine. But something's changed, and I don't understand. I'm worried whether someone else has spoken to her. I have to go and see her, Charlie.'

Charlotte studied her brother's face, seeing the wrinkles etched on his forehead. 'Do you love Emily?' she asked softly. 'Even if she can't trust you?'

'Of course I do. She is my life. I can't believe she left me. She wouldn't even talk to me,' he replied, his voice cracking. 'But I don't know what to do. I don't even know if I can convince her.'

Charlotte pulled him into a hug. They stayed like that for a moment, drawing strength from each other, as the cold hospital light cast long shadows down the hall.

'Whatever happens,' she whispered, 'Greg and I will help you.'

Julien nodded against her shoulder, the tension in his body slowly unravelling.

As they returned to the waiting room, Charlotte was grateful for Greg's reassuring presence nearby. His expression mirrored her anxious thoughts, and when she caught his eye, he approached her.

'We should discuss our trip to France,' he began gently. 'I think we need to postpone it.'

His words tugged at her heart. 'Yes, I thought of that before when I was sitting with Dad. I'll call the school in Lyon and let them know I have to break the contract due to family circumstances,' she replied, her voice shaking slightly.

Greg took her hands in his, squeezing them gently. 'You don't have to face this alone, sweetheart. I'll cancel my flights too. When we go home, I'll do them both.'

Julien's voice broke through their discussion. 'Charlotte, I know this is a big ask,' he began, his eyes dark with concern. 'But seeing you will be here and to allay Dad's worries, would you take over at the store while I'm gone?'

Charlotte felt a lump rise in her throat. She exchanged glances with Greg, who nodded, ready to support her. 'I can, but I don't know anything about it.'

'The staff will help you. They are a great bunch, and they've been fabulous this week. They've all worked extra hours with no complaints while I've been at the hospital.'

Greg put his hand on Julien's shoulder. 'I can help, too, mate—as a friend of the family. I can do the heavy lifting, serve tables, and wash up.'

Overwhelmed, Charlotte reached for Greg as tears spilled down her cheeks.

As they were discussing the details, an alarm

went off in Dad's room, and the nurses hurried in.

Mum came out, her face white. 'It's no good. He's having another attack.' Panic surged through the room as chaos erupted again.

Only a few minutes later, the doctor joined them in the corridor, his expression serious. 'We need to take him into surgery,' he said, his voice firm but calm. 'He's stable for now, but we have to act quickly.'

His words sent shockwaves through the family. Charlotte's mother was already in distress, the fear deepening as her eyes brimmed with tears.

Lisette, Amelia, and Charlotte led their mother slowly toward the family room down the hall, trying to shield her from the medical interactions that were taking place as Dad was prepared for surgery. Meanwhile, Julien and Greg remained behind, facing the realities of the store and what lay ahead.

Julien inhaled deeply, trying to maintain composure as he turned to Greg. 'I honestly don't know how I'll manage everything,' he said, his voice barely above a whisper.

Greg stepped closer, his determination solid.

'You focus on your dad and Emily right now. We'll handle the store.'

EPILOGUE

The General Store

As Charlotte swept the last of the biscuit crumbs into the waste bin, the quiet hum of the General Store enveloped her. The atmosphere felt lighter, almost buoyant. Greg arranged the fresh-baked goods he'd picked up in Maryborough that morning on the counter, his usual easy smile spreading across his face.

'Hey, Charlotte,' he said, glancing over at her. 'Did you hear about the croissants?'

Charlotte rolled her eyes playfully. 'Let me guess, someone else is questioning their authenticity?'

'More than one someone,' he replied with a chuckle. 'A couple of old-timers were discussing how Julien was the croissant king.'

Charlotte laughed, shaking her head. 'Well, we're doing our best here. It's hard to compete with someone like Julien.'

Just then, Amelia breezed into the store, her preschool bag slung over her shoulder. 'You two lovebirds having a moment?' she teased with a raised eyebrow.

'Just discussing pastry politics,' Greg shot back, grinning. 'You know how serious that can get around here.'

'Very serious,' Amelia agreed, leaning against the counter, her expression shifting to one of genuine concern. 'How's Dad doing? Still improving?'

'Yes, Mum called an hour ago,' Charlotte replied, her voice softening. 'Mum's with him as much as she can be. Grandmère and Papa are in Brisbane, too. I think it's helping them all to have each other's company.'

'Good. I hope he knows how many people care about him,' Amelia said, a hint of worry etched in her features.

'He definitely does,' Greg assured her, stepping closer to Charlotte's side. 'And the whole town is rallying behind you guys. Business has been brisk because of it.'

Amelia smiled, but then a playful smirk crossed her face. 'So, when do we get to hear all the romantic details from you two? Have you already picked out your wedding venue?'

Charlotte felt her cheeks heat up. 'Amelia! Oh, please! Not here!'

'I think it's sweet,' Greg interrupted, tightening his arm around Charlotte's waist. 'But I think we'll hold off on wedding plans until we've settled your dad's health concerns.'

'Aw, how practical of you!' Amelia laughed before changing the subject. 'I have to head back to the preschool soon, but let me know if you need extra hands in the store later. I can swing by.'

'Will do,' Charlotte said warmly. 'Thanks for always helping out.'

As Amelia turned to head out, Greg leaned down and whispered to Charlotte, 'Let's take a quick breather in the back. I need a minute away from all this—and I think you do too.'

Charlotte smiled, her heart lightening, and she nodded. They slipped out to the back of the store, leaning against the cool brick wall.

'Thank you once again for helping,' Charlotte murmured, resting her head on Greg's shoulder. The worry of recent events began to lift ever so slightly.

'It's not a chore, Charlotte,' he replied, warmth flooding through him as he squeezed her tighter. 'I'm doing it because I love you—and I'm going to love your family too.'

She looked up at him, her smile radiant as they shared a quick kiss, a promise of their bond growing stronger.

'Ready to head back?' he asked, brushing a strand of hair behind her ear.

'Almost. Just give me a second,' she said, enjoying the moment.

As they walked back into the store, Greg's eyes opened wider when he spotted his parents inside. 'There's Mum and Dad!' he exclaimed.

Charlotte turned and smiled, knowing Greg hadn't seen them in a couple of weeks. 'They must've come to visit,' she said, returning his enthusiasm.

Greg approached them, his heart full. 'Hey! It's great to see you both!'

'Greg, sweetheart!' his mother said, pulling him into a tight embrace. 'You've been doing so much. We're proud of you.'

'Thanks, Mum,' he said, his voice muffled against her shoulder. When he finally pulled back, he glanced at Charlotte, who was watching the family reunion with affection.

'Greg has really helped, you know,' Charlotte said with a smile. 'With everything going on, we wouldn't have managed without his help.'

'Well, it's a team effort,' Greg insisted. 'And I'm loving it. I might change my mind about that law degree, Dad,' he teased.

'It's your choice, son. It's good to see you, Charlotte. I've heard so much about the wonderful job your brother is doing here.'

Charlotte smiled bashfully. 'We're just a quick fill-in until Dad is back on his feet and Julien comes home.'

'We're really pleased to hear your Dad's recovering well,' Greg's mother said.

Greg escorted his parents to a table by the window, the scent of fresh coffee and baked goods wafting through the air. He settled them comfortably before heading back to the counter to place their order.

'Two coffees and a slice of that chocolate cake with two plates, please!' he said to Charlotte, giving her a playful wink. 'Make sure to give them the good stuff.'

Charlotte laughed as she prepared the order, her heart warm from the moment with Greg and the reassurance that her father was off the danger list. It was good to see his parents here, too. The only worry was Julien and whether he could convince Emily of the truth.

She paused for a moment, looking out over the main street of Duckinwilla Creek. The sun shone brightly, illuminating the familiar buildings and the gentle flow of life around her.

When Greg returned to her side, he noticed her gaze fixed outside. 'What are you thinking about?' he asked.

She turned to him, happiness almost overwhelming her. 'Just taking it all in, I guess. It feels . . . right being here. Coming home was the right thing to do. Dad's doing better, Mum's settled, and I think I'm here to stay.'

Greg put his arms around her. 'It's amazing how things have turned around. You should be feeling really happy right now.'

Charlotte nodded as a rush of love for this man flooded through her. 'I do. Your support has made all the difference, and everything has fallen into place. The store is thriving, and most importantly, I have you here with me.'

His gaze softened, and she could see the depth of his feelings in his eyes. 'We're going to build something beautiful together.'

She breathed in deeply, feeling light and hopeful. 'Whatever the future holds, I can face it with you beside me.'

'Absolutely,' he replied. He dropped a quick kiss on her lips. 'I can't believe we're here together.'

Greg's parents waved him over from their table. 'Where's our cake, lovebirds?' his mother called, a broad grin on her face.

'Coming, Mum!' Greg said, kissing Charlotte again before he picked up the order.

As he walked away, happiness suffused Charlotte. She was looking forward to her new future, side by side with the man she loved.

Coming in February

Book 2: Secrets and Surprises

Julien Johnson never planned to stay in Duckinwilla Creek until Emily Dysart followed him home.

With dreams of becoming a renowned city chef, Julien always expected to stay in the city. But when his father retires, leaving Julien to run the family store, he reluctantly agrees to stay—and unexpectedly finds himself happier as he and Emily settle into the rhythms of small-town life. But accusations and whispers of scandal surface, threatening his newfound happiness as he untangles the truth; Julien must face the secrets of his past, prioritise his ambitions, and face the complicated dynamics of a town that never forgets.

Will his choices cost him everything he's come to love, or will they open the door to a life he never dared to dream?

Book 2: Secrets and Surprises

https://annieseatonstore.ecwid.com/Secrets-and-Surprises-Pre-order-March-2025-p707719390

ALSO BY ANNIE SEATON

Daughters of the Darling
From Across the Sea
Over the River
By the Billabong (2025)

A Bec Whitfield Mystery
Bowen River
Shadows on the Shore (June 2025)

Duckinwilla Days
Coming Home
Secrets and Surprises
Books 3-6 to follow in 2025

Home to the Outback *(2025)*
Lucy
Angie
Jemima
Isabella

Porter Sisters Series
Kakadu Sunset
Daintree
Diamond Sky
Hidden Valley
Larapinta
Kakadu Dawn

Others
Whitsunday Dawn
Undara
Osprey Reef
East of Alice

COMING HOME

One Summer in Tuscany
Four Seasons Short and Sweet
Follow the Sun
Ten Days in Paradise
Deadly Secrets
Adventures in Time
Silver Valley Witch
The Emerald Necklace
A Clever Christmas
Christmas with the Boss
Her Christmas Star
The Emerald Necklace

The Augathella Girls Series
Outback Roads
Outback Sky
Outback Escape
Outback Wind
Outback Dawn
Outback Moonlight
Outback Dust
Outback Hope
Boxed Sets
Augathella Girls 1-4
Augathella Girls 5-8

Augathella Short and Sweet Series
An Augathella Surprise
An Augathella Baby
An Augathella Spring
An Augathella Christmas
An Augathella Wedding
An Augathella Easter
An Augathella Masquerade Ball
Boxed Set
Augathella Short and Sweet 1-3

ANNIE SEATON

Sunshine Coast Series
Waiting for Ana
The Trouble with Jack
Healing His Heart
Sunshine Coast Boxed Set

The Richards Brothers Series
The Trouble with Paradise
Marry in Haste
Outback Sunrise
Richards Brothers Boxed Set

Bondi Beach Love Series
Beach House
Beach Music
Beach Walk
Beach Dreams
The House on the Hill Boxed Set

Second Chance Bay Series
Her Outback Playboy
Her Outback Protector
Her Outback Haven
Her Outback Paradise
Boxed Set-The McDougalls of Second Chance Bay

Love Across Time Series
Come Back to Me
Follow Me
Finding Home
The Threads that Bind
Boxed Set
Love Across Time 1-4

COMING HOME

Bindarra Creek
Worth the Wait
Full Circle
Secrets of River Cottage
A Clever Christmas
A Place to Belong

Annie lives in Australia, on the beautiful north coast of New South Wales. She sits in her writing chair and looks out over the tranquil Pacific Ocean.

She writes contemporary romance and loves telling stories that always have a happily ever after. She lives with her very own hero of many years and they share their home with Barney, the rag doll puss, who hides when the four grandchildren come to visit.

Stay up to date with her latest releases at her website: **http://www.annieseaton.net**

If you would like to stay up to date with Annie's releases, subscribe to her newsletter here: http://www.annieseaton.net

www.ingramcontent.com/pod-product-compliance
Ingram Content Group UK Ltd.
Pitfield, Milton Keynes, MK11 3LW, UK
UKHW041411180426
11947UKWH00007B/59